Graziano Urli

THE CASE OF FRIULIAN HAMLET

Story occurred in London, on a tenth of August of the new millennium

AT SAINT JAMES HOSTEL

Lying on the bed at Saint James hostel, Earls Court, I'm trying to sleep a spell, but there are so many things on this day, tensions, roaming about my mind. In the early morning I left Codroipo on the train to Treviso, and then on the Ryanair flight to London, so full as a tin of sardines. At Treviso airport queuing for the check in, for security where they grope you everywhere. Take off your shoes, put your laptop in the bin, and my smartphone where the devil has it gone? In my jacket, how stupid! What do they want now? Maybe I laughed at them and they want to make it clear they give orders. 'Take off your shoes again and give us your documents.' The Italians, too, start fucking around now!

On the plane the stewards kept moving up and down: the aperitif, the snack, duty free perfumes, the lottery, the tickets for London theaters, museums and who knows what? It isn't a good job. They might get some extra money, a percentage on what they sell. The time had gone when those who flew Alitalia used to stay three days in New York, before coming back. Intercontinental flights weariness, the jet lag, risky work, retired at forty. Not stupid! Now they too are going through a rough patch.

Quite right as far as Stansted Airport, but then on the train to Victoria Station they played a first bad joke on me. Almost a fatal blow to the little money supply I had brought with me from home with the idea of surviving one week in London. Fifteen quid! Thieves! Too late to look for something alternative and tired without doing anything. If there had been four, five of us, we might have taken a black taxi, the Austin Morris, as in the school trip.

Everybody crammed behind to save money.

'Damned Italians!' grumbled the taxi driver thinking we wouldn't understand him.

The man who sleeps in the bunk bed under me arrived at the dormitory not long ago, he threw himself on to the bed and fell asleep immediately.

A stench of wine to vomit. He started snoring to move the sheet which dangled below my bed.

The man who sleeps above was already there when I entered the dormitory and hasn't moved since then. A heap of rags. I tried to stand on tiptoe to see if he was sleeping, or pretending, or he was a dead body as in the movies. I went nearer to see if he was sleeping. The hardly perceptible movement of his shoulders rising and descending with his breath. Thank goodness! He was still alive.

At the hostel reception they played the second bad joke on me.

'In advance!' said the clerk.

I won't have much money left if I have to pay the whole week in advance. She didn't mind: 'Either this way or you get out of here.'

Then she gave me a form of sheet that as soon as I entered the dormitory 'two-five', without a bit of light, with the man above I didn't know whether he was awake or stiff dead, it took me ages to see which was the right or the reverse side. In hostels it is always so hot, in summer and winter, to keep the sash window a bit open, with the continuous noise of the city outside, and to listen to that devil of buzz which never stops a moment with the ambulance siren far away. A serious risk to get to the nearest hospital in traffic jams. Better the helicopter (HEMS) which takes a moment to arrive, but then where does it land in London? That is the problem. The police siren has stopped just across the hostel street. They might have brought in some pimps I hope, with the bunch of young women in the streets, lots of orientals, you can't understand where they are from, all the same, Siamese, Burmese … It is not called so their country any more, Myanmar, something like that. They were everywhere. A black, young woman even got near me outside Victoria Station.

'I love you!' she said to me.

'Me too, dear, but what about the money? Doggone it, I haven't got any!' I showed her my pockets and shrugged a little. She began to laugh and told me something I didn't understand. It is difficult to figure English out if you don't use the right intonation. Who knows where they take their clients. At the hostel, that would be convenient, maybe at a YMCA, that is, a Christian association for boys. For young women, they agree at a reasonable price. Of course twin beds, also etiquette has its importance.

Ffrrr Ffrrr … Damn! It's the smartphone on vibrate mode. Where did it end up? In the rucksack at the bottom of the bed. I guess it is Carmela who's calling me on her mobile phone. Shit! I forgot phoning her in Friuli. Was it necessary? Here, everything's fine, accommodation, company, peace and quiet, right now she had to call me that the two thieves, above and below, were sleeping. If I had to roll out of bed one of the two, I'd roll out the stinker below, damned for eternity, but with these chaps it is better to forget it, to God the Last Judgment.

Luckily I've got a short message ready in the store. 'I'm fine.' One click and go!

There! The alcoholic bomb below has woken up, and after hawking and spitting quickly to the bathroom to puke everything. While he's emptying out, let's check the phone. Here it is. She isn't happy. She might be right, but well? … What are you going to do in London? I've got so many things to do, you don't know the language and so on with this spiel. Now, not even a message to say everything's okay, where I am and with whom. Always that obsession in her head, who knows who is consoling him tonight? Champagne and cotillons, women galore, well London. Sometimes it looks like a show, something in the air, the baseless fabric of a vision. So, to hint she's angry, but sure she always finds something to do in company, in and out of home. She isn't short of female friends and of some male friends too, I wish it weren't so! She always gets lots of compliments from those who work with her. The executive director of the firm is a perfect man, he isn't lacking in anything, a handsome man. He stirs me, he turns me on. Women! Let's send this message before the drunkard comes out of the bathroom. Here he is. Luckily he sleeps below, otherwise he might kill himself to go to the top of a bunk bed. Experience helps somehow. Maybe it is also written in the hostel rules. The bunks below for those over sixty-five, drunkards and so on, with a little addition of five pounds. They are the ones which sell out fast when there are football matches, or when the darlings of black blocs come to visit, and use the bunks above to put their armament: cudgels, helmets, slings and everything they need to raise hell, and then go about to brag. They might have a decent nest egg to pay for a good hotel, a fair pocket money, or dad's card. Who knows whether something has changed since P.P. Pasolini used to say they are always the same chaps who make a din, children of wealthy middle class, a bit fed up because they don't know what to do, a bit bloody-minded against their fathers who keep warm the best employments as pharmacist, lawyer, notary, the insurance, the estate agency, the car dealership and so on. Unruly sons, though ready to enter the system again when it suits them. Maybe now in that list there are also mingled all those who have lost their job, or those who have never had it, not to mention the troop of illegal immigrants, invisible, shadows who live with us. In the morning they give you a hand to park the car, they wait for you outside the supermarket for the euro, at traffic lights to clean your car windows, they ring your doorbell to sell you who knows what, to wake you up at night for a quick look at your house. No, thank you. Next time.

You can never guess the time in a hostel in the early morning. In London above all, when it is cloudy, with buildings close to other buildings. You don't know whether it is pitch dark or it has started to get light. Not even a bell tower to hear the clock strike the hours and the quarters of the hour to make you nervous when you are about to fall asleep. The drunkards who yell down in the street are not a good clock. They never want to go to sleep, and if full like a barrel, they might place themselves below the window to argue, to swear, to sing. The whole world's a bottle, a life's but a dram when the bottle gets empty, it sure ain't worth a damn.

Pspspsps … Oh, God, is it the tap of the man above which spills? He is dreaming loud, or, maybe, wait … It is as though he's whispering the lesson for school. Maths test tomorrow with that teacher, poor soul. What a nightmare! Who knows why almost all Maths teachers are women? It should be the opposite, with their brain inclined to languages, fact more than obvious. Maybe they do it on purpose to confuse teenagers' ideas already quite muddled.

Spspspspsp, Jesus, he's praying. He might be a Moroccan who must pray when the sun rises and sets, and also before going to bed. In Marrakesh, they were all in the mosque at ten, eleven in the evening, only male, women in front of the telly or knitting, before hiding themselves under the blankets, where they well know how to win respect. I wonder whether you can pray in bed or you must do it on the carpet towards the rising sun. Towards the door? I am not that sure. I'd better be quiet, never disturb someone's praying. He might kill you for faith. Longing for Heaven, together with the nice soul of Beatrix, who well knows the oldest dances. Watch out! He put his feet dangling out of the bed. Perfumed like those of pilgrims in Coena Domini with Pope Francis. Are they black? You can't say it in the dark. Young, seeing how he jumped down from above and a nice build, like a strapping fellow to the bathroom. I'll check the time on the phone. Four. What a bore! What a drag! Time never passes and I haven't slept a wink. There's no light from the window. Always the same reddish color behind the pane of the town asleep. Unreal city. I'm looking in vain for a glimmer of light among the flashes of some rare cars which dart away in the night. How difficult it is to struggle on! Who can get asleep by now? As soon as the Moroccan comes in, I'll rush into the bathroom. I might go about the corridors to look for one which is free. Anyway, at this time they are all in bed. I don't want to get lost in the degraded labyrinths of the hostel, without a bit of light, or to have an unpleasant encounter.

Who knows whether that chap's coming back or he's gone on an errand around the dormitories. It is an unpretentious hostel, still, you can scrape together something all the same, if you know what to do. He isn't back, I'll carefully get up myself trying not to put my feet on the one below, then, I'd be in trouble. Let's hope he's cooled off a bit. Slowly, first one foot, then the other, the wooden floor which creaks under my feet, the door which squeaks on the hinges and I'm out. A beam of light through the bathroom door ajar and nobody inside. The miserable English bathroom with the filthy carpet, a big bathtub without a shower dating back to queen Victoria, and not even a hanger for clothes, a tap for hot water, another for cold water and I defy a man to wash himself in that filth. What demands! Sure, it isn't the Hilton Hotel, with the little money the president of the association gave to me. Order of payment by the Committee for Friulian Hamlet, signed by the secretary.

SPECIAL MISSION IN LONDON

Sitting on the toilet, at Earls Court Saint James hostel, a few minutes after four in the morning, I'm thinking of my strange mission in London, how my story began, two weeks ago.

'For a special errand,' said the president of the Committee for Friulian Hamlet on the phone.

On a short-term contract all my life, I rushed to see him in his Codroipo office. He immediately started with his ceremonies.

'You've studied... Who knows the language better than you? You'll go to London to speak to this university teacher who is retired now. He was the most important collaborator of Cecil Clough, the eminent academic of Shakespeare, who after years of research stated that the sources of the tragedy *Romeo and Juliet* are not to look into the feud between two families in the city of Verona, but it is totally a Friulian matter, occurred in the context of the Peasants' Revolt of Shrove Thursday, on the twenty-seventh of February, fifteen eleven,' the president explained.

'I still remember professor Clough's speech,' he continued. 'Here it is. I'll make you a copy from the magazine *Il Ponte*.'

The magazine reported professor Clough's whole speech. I put on my glasses and quietly read a little part of his lecture.

'The passionate story of the two young people in love, Luigi da Porto, alias Romeo Montague, and Lucina Savorgnan, alias Juliet Capulet, occurred in Udine in February fifteen eleven. The two youths met on a terrible night, a night of violence in Friuli, and fell in love at first sight. Not long afterwards, Luigi was wounded in battle and abandoned by his beloved. However, he never forgot Lucina, and decided to write his heart-breaking story, the genius of Shakespeare transformed into something universal.

Everywhere you go, they know Romeo and Juliet. Everybody knows the masterpiece of this tragic love. Everywhere you go, they know Verona, the town of this universal love story, but don't know Udine, the place where the true events happened, and they don't know the two Friulians, Luigi and Lucina, the real protagonists of the tragedy.'

However, afterwards, this matter didn't go so well, because Friulians are good people, and instead of marketing, instead of finding a cozy balcony in the center of Udine, with a vine which creeps up to the first floor, a nice writing in grand style, *Casa Savorgnan*, alias Capuleti, the Friulians remained quiet. They might have called the extras from Palmanova, specialist in historic commemorations. And from the balcony above, a Friulian beauty:

'What's in a name? That which we call a rose, by any other name would smell as sweet ...'

Every Sunday, soon after the Mass, from early spring till the end of the summer festival, Halloween for younger people, when you could have imagined a fancy-dress ball with fifteenth century costumes and masks, witches, ghosts galore, and sure free chestnuts and ribolla wine for everybody. You didn't need a committee for this idea, but why putting into the field such eccentricities? We are Friulians! Why are they coming to bother us? We are fine this way.

'Guglielmo, you'll wonder why I called you here,' the president continued. 'What I've told you now is the past. A story almost forgotten. Today's great news is the research done by Cecil Clough's collaborator and friend on the sources of Shakespeare's greatest tragedy, *Hamlet*.

'Yes, but what does Codroipo have to do with Shakespeare's *Hamlet*?' I asked him more and more curious.

'What a hurry! Wait, and I'll tell you!' the president answered back lifting his arm quite irritated. 'Not really Codroipo, but I've got good reasons to think of the small community of Camino al Tagliamento. In fact, professor Ben Brough, from his London old people's home, asserts with proved documents that Shakespeare to write *Hamlet* made reference to Rizzardo the Second da Camino, marquis of Treviso, maybe killed by his brother Guecellone in thirteen twelve,' said the president with raising enthusiasm.

'I can't understand the connection between the marquis da Camino in the Middle Ages and the small community of Camino al Tagliamento,' I pointed out a bit dubious.

'You are right, the da Camino were marquises in Treviso, but they had always aspired to annex Aquileia Patriarchate to their March. And Camino, the most beautiful village in Friuli, must have been tempting Trevisan marquises, or else why calling it Camino and not something else?'

Very happy of his analysis, the president came to me, seized my arm, and, as if to confide a great secret to me, he whispered in my ear.

'The most disturbing fact is that of Camino old miller's nephew, Amlêt. Do you remember him? He went about saying he was a prince of the da Camino family. The damned prince, he shouted loud, the last descendant of the important family of the Lords da Camino, in the Middle Ages, cursed lineage, stained by Cain's guilt, the murder of his brother Abel.'

When the president mentioned Amlêt, I didn't remember him any more. I had completely forgotten him. Disappeared two years ago, somebody says he's dead, maybe he wasn't so insane, when he went to the pubs to tell people he was a prince. Everybody in the village made fun of him when he went around to show the seal of the da Camino family, a silver ring, coat of arms of Trevisan marquises, found who knows where. They laughed behind his back and called him prince charming, with contempt. They paid him to drink in the pubs to see him rave. 'Something is rotten in the *Patria del Friuli*,' he shouted when he was dead drunk. Poor youth! I remember he also took private lessons from me, always with the obsession that people didn't treat him with the respect due to a prince.

Fallen even more into a depression, he kept drinking and, after two hospitalizations with cirrhosis of the liver, he vanished into thin air. He went to his ancestors' homeland, to die beneath the castle ruins of Trevisan marquises, drown in the river Sile and gone for ever, the villagers from Camino with a little schooling kept saying for a while. Till professor Brough came out with this evidence regarding Shakespeare's *Hamlet*. An old scholar's fixation, or Shakespeare cared about Friuli more than the Friulians themselves, who say around the Friulian language doesn't count shit, and you just need to know English?

'Two coincidences are a clue,' said the president. 'At this point, we members of the Committee couldn't draw back, because the matter could be a great opportunity of promotion of the territory. After a council meeting, the assembly appointed me to attend to the case and see what professor Brough's idea was.'

When the news became public, you can imagine the gossip in the small community of Camino, not only in pubs and in the street, but also on socials, in the paper Il Messaggero and on television. The more informed immediately speculated that *Elsinore*, Hamlet's castle, must have been between the villages of Stracis and Bugnins, at least this was the opinion of the Bar Sport. However, the more learned came up with Latin, *'Elsinore buscus ut extensa Varamus usque ad Tilimentum,'* because they argued that sure, Shakespeare was peculiar, but still he couldn't set his most important tragedy in Stracis or Bugnins, or else I wonder what clever ideas the great masters of Friulian toponymy would have produced in their meetings.

After accepting the idea of coming to England to speak to professor Brough, and after setting all the details, I was leaving when the president came to me and put one hand on my shoulder.

'In confidence, I'll tell you something I shouldn't tell anybody, professional secrecy,' he muttered. 'The marshal of the Carabinieri revealed to me they are investigating with carbon-fourteen!'

Then he hid his mouth with one hand and told me softly in my ear, 'They've found some human bones wrapped in cellophane under the Cadoro supermarket, with a writing in block letters, HAM! Goddamn! They're the initials of *Hamlet* in English, aren't they?'

'Sure!'

'Two coincidences are a clue, three coincidences are a proof. Guglielmo, go quickly to London that afterwards we'll give you a permanent employment as deputy president of the Committee!'

I didn't dare tell the poor man that it might have been a chunk of San Daniele ham for export, rotten to the core, placed in a plastic wrap so that it didn't reek, and then forgotten for future memory. I have always considered ignorance a delicate exotic fruit, touch it and the bloom is gone.

Going back from the bathroom to the dormitory is like coming out of Knossos labyrinth without Ariadne's thread. To the right, to the left, you never understand where to turn, and if there was a bit of light to see the numbers … That's all I need now to start shouting for help. At last, here is the number two-one, and if there is two-one, there must be two-five as well. Move on Savoia! That explains the benefit of orienteering courses on the first day at high school.

I think I can see a glimmer of light coming from outside. The day's breaking. I don't feel like trying to sleep in that pigsty. I'll get inside quietly to take my clothes, and away about the city, free to exist.

Two-five, let's see whether the knob turns to open the door. An odor you can't breathe, and they are not lilies. In order not to die intoxicated in that stench, quickly I'll grab my tracksuit, my jeans, the rucksack with the papers and the money left, if they haven't cleaned it out, as it happened when I was a boy in the holiday home of Fratis in the mountains. They always stole everything from the dormitories, and if you reported it to the assistants, they beat you up, those bullies from Torrimpietra. What bullying! They straighten your back, they help you grow up, you'll see in the national service! Thus, the expert educators of Friulian neolithic comforted you. They even stole my catechism book I had brought from home to revise those lousy notions. My family disgrace, I even resat the catechism exam that unhappy year. Where's God? Taking care of my bike so that they can't steal it. What was worse, though, they even pinched the Milan club cards, with Gianni Rivera, the little abbot, and Pierino Prati, the pest. Really, I cried my heart out for that loss, the dearest thing I had. Before leaving for Fratis, my mother went to buy the postcards and the stamps to send home with the good news from the holiday camp.

'Why don't you write me a few lines now, in order that I may just post them?' I suggested to her.

'But, what shall I write?' she wondered, quite perplexed.

'I eat well and have even put on two kilos.'

A situation which never occurred, on the contrary, with wonder I came home even skinnier. However, I was not the only one who suffered in that awful place because of stress and dejection. One of my mates, aged eight, even escaped from the miserable place and started running downhill for kilometers along the Pontebbana. They found him crying desperately, sitting on a stone by the side of the road. After caning him harshly, they sent him home on the first coach.

The Moroccan above is also back from the rounds and peeking at me. He even makes me feel a sense of discomfort, poor soul. He might be thinking where is this chap going with the city still shrouded in darkness? And now off to the exploration of London without the traffic and confusion of the rush hour.

The employee at the reception peers at me askance.

'Where the devil are you coming from?'

'Dormitory two-five.'

A glance at the papers.

'Guglielmo?'

'Yes, it's me.'

'Okay.' And quietly, not to be heard: 'Fuck Italians, never keep their place!'

You need to understand what you are asked, and not to do like my brother-in-law at JFK security. He was locked up for an hour, the worst in his life, because he couldn't explain to a tanned policeman, evil eyes, what he was doing in New York and where he'd booked to sleep.

MORNING AT HYDE PARK

Outside dawn is breaking. Thank goodness! I might pass for somebody who's walking to work with quick steps, or, in the dark, the invisible souls of the night stop you at each crossroads, and it is risky to turn your back on them and pretend you don't see. You might come across a bastard who pulls out a knife. 'I too have to eat and my young children, my pregnant wife and grandma in a wheelchair.' You always have to keep a banknote of ten pounds ready, or fifty if it is not enough.

Nobody can imagine how beautiful it is roaming around London at daybreak on a beautiful summer day. Just few cars whiz along the wide avenues in the center, but down the most secluded, narrow alleys there's nobody around. A few elderly people gaze at me from the window ajar, a bobby has glimpsed me at a certain distance. He keeps an eye on me, where I'm going. I must quicken my step, pretend I don't mean harm, that I've got a reason to go about London so early in the morning, and not to turn round and look at him. They have to control and not the opposite.

It's five in the morning, on the tenth of August in London. Just a cool breeze, but you feel fine outside when you can't sleep. It's like being rekindled, coming to life again, and you thank God to be born, you feel better and would like to do something for this wicked world. Hyde Park might be the ideal place to spend some time in the morning before breakfast. Through Kensington Borough, it's the shortest way to get to the park. So many small haunts, meeting-places for the night, bars, clubs to enjoy a bit this miserable life of ours. A binge, a blast to put a patch on the void we've got inside. Weird people who budge in and out of a local, tired from the night revelry, a mix of human mankind. From the whore with her last cigarette, long legs slouching in a swivel chair in front of the bar, who is giving me a blank stare, to the people sleeping on the divan behind, to other chaps, with their heads propped up on the elbow leaned on the bar, who stare at me without seeing me. Everything inside gives a sense of dirt, of neglect, and outside down the high-street, in a loud noise, seven, eight men are coming ahead behind the dustcart. They collect the muck of the night which has almost given way to a new day.

Hyde Park seems to be a place out of the world. All nature enjoys the peace of early morning. In the Serpentine a row of ducklings are chasing each other, and the warbling of a black bird gives me the impression of being alone in this world. London. The few people I run into greet me, smile at me and nod their farewell. When the rising sun pierces the haze, I feel like being a child again, running after the squirrel which teasingly places itself in front of me, or a little bird which avoids me by an inch for the haste of feeding its littluns.

All the great city seems to wear the beauty of the morning. The houses of Belgravia seem asleep and the palaces kindle, luminous, resplendent, in the fresh, crystal sky of the morning, all bright and glittering in the smokeless air.

I'm sitting on a bench with the wish this moment won't end any more, may last forever, but the mighty heart of the city is awaiting to start again, and in a moment everything will be different. I don't want to rise from here any more, my eyes are closing of fatigue. I want to sleep, I want to die so, on a beautiful summer morning in London.

The bell of the Immaculate Church, towards Piccadilly, is

playing the Ave Maria. The sound is coming from far away with the city which is awakening. It isn't a dream, it's six in the morning in London.

MORNING IN CAMINO

The tolling of the Ave Maria spreads about the countryside of Camino al Tagliamento when Carmela comes back home. Nobody is waiting for her. She looks at herself in the mirror of the bathroom: her strained face without expression, her little, tired eyes. Everything shows the burden of years, but it's better not to think, and with a nice sleep everything will be the same again. Who can get to sleep now, after such an evening spent with my dear director? Really, he didn't want to let me go. He came from behind, all excited, while I was finishing work at the computer. He put his hand on my shoulder and caressed it softly. Around fifty, the same age as Guglielmo, but a completely different nature, other passion. By the way, let me see whether he's written a sms from London the poor chap of my husband. 'Everything's okay.' Sure, he doesn't bother to write more or to call me. It is his character. Better this way, he lives longer and lets me live as well. Too tired for the prayer. Maybe the Act of Pain, *I am heartily sorry* ... Luckily tomorrow I won't go to work, I'll spend time making love. Well said. I was getting ready to go home. He quietly entered my office and closed the door behind.

'Carmela, I'd have something important to tell you about the next fair.' He suddenly put his hands on my hips. He smiled brightly and drew me closer. Then he kissed me passionately. I shivered, I just broke up. Oh my gosh, I didn't resist my dear director, the womaniser of my director. I remember the first time it happened. I was in the first year of junior secondary at the nuns' boarding school. I repeated the class that year. His name was Paul and was in the third year. That spring we always managed to escape in the afternoon, and used to go across the fields behind the boarding school, looking for a quiet spot. It all happened so quickly. I was underneath, he above me. His hands were exploring all my body. I pulled him tight on me, completely dazed. He opened my tender legs, farewell oh my virginity.

Without parents since I was little, at the boarding school a certain caprice was growing inside me also with the nuns. They called me Shirley Temple, I've never understood why, when I would wiggle my hips in front of them, shaking my head here and there at every step, all a blonde curl. I also liked hugging the novices tightly, letting them caress me, and at night, before getting to sleep, between a Pater-Ave-Glory, to quiet it my tender hand did wonders. I left the boarding school at eighteen when I took up with a married man in his fifties. Full of money, but not so healthy, and I, stupid and young, even took pleasure in humiliating him. He passed away a few years ago, poor chap, and I can't get it out of my head that me too was to blame. After that I met Guglielmo. I had to do everything myself. It was out of the question! He looked at me furtively, shyly. You saw he fancied me, no wonder, he'd never touched a woman! Tell me you love me, yes I do, and on kissing each other at the cinema. They showed *Malice* starring Laura Antonelli. I was so excited. A good man, I've always told him so, and sure I am convinced. The best moments in my life, for ever, I promise I'll be faithful till the end, and love you and honor you all the days in my life. Poor men! It is so hard the concept of family nowadays, of a relationship that lasts the whole life, to see yourself part of another person, his half, *I am Heathcliff,* even more for myself who have never shared anything important with the people I've met in my life. Always fighting, always looking for a personal revenge. Now I'll show you dear! Guglielmo gave me a big hand at the beginning. He made fun of me and called me his sex bomb, but then he, sort of, understood I took all his space, that everything was becoming routine. Surely my aggressive behavior towards men hasn't done him good. *La Belle Dame sans merci thee hath in thrall.* And then it was the loss of our son. A sorrow I've always tried to hide. Now he says to me: 'I must go to London to speak to a professor. I can't take you as well. I'm sure there will be another opportunity.' All right, I'm going out with the director, more annoyance than a wish for revenge, an instinctive desire to return to my former messed-up life, without rules to respect, without disciplined morality. He went back to the life of a single person. A lot of things to do, he says to me, when he comes back angry with his colleagues. And then he locks himself in the lounge to watch television alone. What does a woman like me do with such a man? Only occasional contacts with my life, a cold bed, after we lost the baby. Ten years ago. A life. I was waiting for that child as a gift from God, and it seemed to me I was living somebody else's life, as if a light enveloped me and accompanied me to an unknown fate. I was feeling better. They were beautiful spring days with nature in love, and I too was feeling part of that change in everybody's life, that passage a new birth can conjure up. All people had particular care towards me. Surely, in these situations everybody is alone, and we cope only with the character and the determination we've got inside. I had the impression I could change my life, that it was possible to forget the past and start anew. Now, after ten years everything has returned as before. The spinning

top turns, turns to return to the beginning. The past is always with me, it pushes me back to my childhood, to the malice which helps you face the evil world we've got ahead. I would never have got and I'd never get to the despair of the poor woman who was near me in hospital. She never stopped crying. I think she came from Colombia, but I'm not that sure. I'm about to separate from my husband, she says to me. I knew it wouldn't work, we are so different. It was a sensation, I was feeling that inside. Last year I lost my baby, Marc, five months pregnant. The poor thing wept bitterly also during the night. I wanted that child. I needed Marc. They told me it was a virus taken who knows where around the world. Now, here in hospital, I lost the baby a second time, two months. Poor woman! We can hardly imagine the life of those poor people who come to us, with the hope to start something important. After that, the disappointment. My husband is feeling trapped, malcontent. He wants to go back to Colombia. He's tried so many jobs, but can't stay in one post. Lots of working hours he isn't used to for a miserable salary you can't even buy food. And now we are going to separate. Noooo! I don't want to go back to Colombia with him. I don't know whether I still love him, she confided in me every evening in hospital, crying with sorrow. I'll have to find a job here. I must find a job to pay the rent. Too expensive, but I can't go back to my family in Colombia. They would slam the door in my face, I'm sure. You should listen to what your parents tell you. They know you better than anybody else. I really wanted that baby, Marc. What's happening to me? I don't know what to do any more. Poor me! Poor me!
It is eight in the morning when Carmela falls asleep.

THE MEETING WITH HORATIO

It's six in the morning in London. I'm sitting on a bench in Hyde Park on a cool, beautiful morning in the summer. In front of me, southwards, the beautiful view of the Royal Albert Hall brightened by the first sunlight. A man is coming near.

'May I …?' he asks me.

'Please, sit down!'

In his early sixties, thin, quick, nervous movements, clean-shaven, long, gray hair put in a short tail behind, a checked shirt hopping outside his trousers to emphasize his lean body. He speaks perfect English, and when I tell him I'm Italian, he tries to improvise some sentences with his Spanish knowledge, from his life spent in Mexico to teach English.

He speaks about the good food of that country, about the ten rules to avoid stress, the reason why we are there to spend our time at six in the morning. It makes me think he is a lonely man, that I am a lonely person too. And many people look at me in the face, and stop me in the street to ask for some information, a favor, and maybe they also confide something to me, as when you are hiking in the mountains and you'd like to tell a person you've just met all your life. It might be a matter of eyes that observe, good eyes which try to understand, which contemplate reality with wonder. Some people have it written on their forehead, I am made to rule, and don't be a pain in the arse because I have no time to lose, and then there are people without qualities, so they are called, always ready to give a hand, you look for in case of need. He tells me that he too lives in a hostel, at Phoenix Hostel, near Regent's Park, where he knows the owner who gives him free accommodation and meals for a few hours of work as a receptionist.

Me too in a few years like this man here, without a country, without affections, alone in the world. A situation which is a great temptation, which makes me think about our human condition, with more honesty towards ourselves, about what we are doing here alone, to hear all the confusion surrounding us, the sham, the fluttering about of this human race. Let drop every day in corruption, lies, chatter.

After speaking long about himself, he asks me who I am, whether I do something respectable in my life.

'Yes, I am a scholar,' I say to him.

A professional man, a researcher, a brain in flight. It isn't easy to make yourself understood abroad, when you speak about Italy. How can you explain to him you are a teacher on a short-term contract in your late forties, you work sometimes here, sometimes there, and now in London you are on a mission for the crap of a grotesque committee, and for the vision of a poor, old teacher, now retired? Foolish thing.

'I see, and … what's your important mission here in London?' he asks me.

Sure, on a mission from God. What bullshit I'll tell him now? Sure, I'm not John Belushi. And why not telling him the truth? Also a painful truth, paradoxical, ridicule might reveal something important about human nature, strutting on stage for an hour before the great silence.

I explain to him the research on the sources of Shakespeare's theater.

'Shakespeare? My passion, my love, my everything...' the man proclaims in a sort of ecstasy.

The enthusiasm of the man urges me to tell him about *Romeo and Juliet,* about *Hamlet,* but it is just a short interval, because it always happens to me to find somebody who pushes me aside, who gets on his high horse, and my idea, my project becomes inconsistent, till it vanishes altogether, to give way to the knowledge of those who always have an answer, who clearly see ahead where they're going, or simply they want to fill a void, and move quickly in a world of shadows.

But this man here really knows something about *Hamlet,* he isn't like our political braggart who just to show how good he is, he also risks some sentences in English. De, de, de … He tells me he's acted Shakespeare since his childhood, he always used him in his classes.

'Mercutio was my last role as an actor,' he says to me.

'I talk of dreams, which are the children of an idle brain, begot of nothing but vain fantasy,' he quotes from *Romeo and Juliet.*

'Are you still acting?' I ask him.

'Not any more now.' After that last audition, he was told he was too old.

'Obsolete. They might have been right,' he admits.

But how to accept the fact when one thinks he's still got a lot to do? And he might also be right, because those who push to enter surely don't have his knowledge, his experience. He doesn't say it, maybe he doesn't think it either. He stops speaking for a moment and looks deeply into my eyes as to see whether I share his opinion.

'Are you with me?' he inquires.

Maybe experience and knowledge are trivialities in a world which runs too fast. What kind of experience and knowledge a man who was young more than fifty years ago might have, when values were so different? Just inconsistent opinions. And yet, in a world whose population is getting older and older, we'll have to find a solution to avoid a conflict between generations. What blame does an elderly man have to get old? The gray vote, the right to vote for those who have gray hair and live too long. The public opinion thinks the world has changed and they, the elderly, mustn't have the right to decide for the young. For those who travel the world, brain drain, like migratory birds which fly free, without gravity, and land where their fancy leads them. They also have the sat nav with them for the shortest way, the less congested, the one where you don't pay duty. Lots of them stay at home, without a job, little money in their pocket, just what dad gives to them.

Our five-starred Grillo, a comedian in the old days, now become a laughing-stock himself, would like to pass a bill on the scrapping of the elderly, and in England they've returned to Malthus theories, two hundred years ago. For him the epidemics were God's grace to limit the growth of the population. In line with him lots of English people think that to tackle pandemics we'll have to get to herd immunity, with the result that to fall ill and die and disappear from this world are the weaker, the elderly. Don't even count the Germans who always have extreme remedies. We mustn't gas the aged, sure! What blame do they have if they live longer, with the reminder of medication which rings every hour. The pill for the heart, that for high-blood pressure, to hear well, to see better, to resurrect lust and maybe the little tablet for grandmas who want to give birth to children at sixty, now that we have the demographic crisis. The real problem would be pensions: there wouldn't be money for everybody. Money might be printed, but if there is no food, what's the use of it? We should invent injections which suppress appetite. Doctors say the elderly must eat healthily: soft cheese and a lot of season vegetables, and drink plenty of good mineral water, at least two liters a day, which makes you piss, and eat fruit, bananas above all, and a small glass of good red wine at meals. Too demanding the old chaps! We can't make it. We need to agree with God Almighty. We might send him the most sickly old boys and those over seventy. For those, He Himself will provide. He feeds and gives them something to do, because it is no good to stay doing nothing. Little things, of course. What do I know? If in this world he was a good electrician, he might check the Paradise lights, if he was a bad electrician, he might service the Hell conditioners a bit. Instead, if he was a good dairyman, he might prepare low-fat cheese which helps levitation, if he was a bad dairyman, he might make cheese with worms, and from time to time bank up a fire under the cauldron. If he was a bad cook, he might prepare rice with poisonous mushrooms, instead, if he was a holy cook, he might make good things, that anyway in Heaven we don't risk putting on weight. Though, Almighty God too might not be very happy to have only old chaps and would also desire some callow lass. And then, I'm afraid He too hasn't got much room over there. Chinese and Indians have always given Him problems, without considering He's still trying to put up those who were wiped out by the Germans, let's not include those who were exterminated by the communists, it can't be helped, nobody can find them. Who knows? They might have found the way to reincarnate because nobody speaks, nobody writes about them.

My new acquaintance has suddenly stopped speaking. He might have understood I was not following him any more, entered my secret world, the parallel world, the boundless sea where I like losing myself. *Dolce il naufragar in questo mare.* He's realized he stole my space. It doesn't happen so often in every day's reality to find so sensitive people. It is usually a crazy race ahead to show off how good we are, what superior intelligence God Almighty gave to us! He doesn't have to apologize. We are here in this world trying to leave a sign, maybe a faint memory, a recollection, not to be forgotten. And we always go back to the most beautiful moments in our life, when we believed in something really important. We like living those moments again, also a bit more beautiful in our imagination, maybe raised to a halo of holiness.

How lovely this tranquility in Hyde Park is, when two people realize that something important is about to begin.

The clock of Piccadilly bell tower strikes seven and I understand that this retired professor, this former actor of Shakespeare, will accompany me during my London trip looking for professor Brough, to the discovery of the mystery of Friulian Hamlet.

'My name's Horatio,' he presents himself without ceremonies to resume the conversation.

'I am Guglielmo. So pleased to meet you!'

'Me too. Nice to make your acquaintance.' With a vigorous handshake to share the special moment we're living.

Horatio, Hamlet's friend in the tragedy by Shakespeare, the first who saw the ghost of the old king. *If thou hast any sound, or use of voice, speak to me...* Ideal character to get in touch with afterlife.

At dusk, down the river banks outside Camino al Tagliamento, a dense fog you could cut with a knife, till the old miller's ruined house, Amlêt's grandfather, the young man gone as a drifter, vanished into thin air and never returned. The matter is getting rather entangled, shrouded in a world of mystery, of nightmares running with the shadows of the night.

Horatio makes me feel less alone in my mission here in London. He taught all over the world and then returned home, to the city of his youth. Full of memories, but also inwardly rich to continue his life itinerary, trying to share something with free souls, wild spirits like him, who can never keep still in one place, who are never overwhelmed by the world malaise, don't care about the scorn of time which passes so fast, old without realizing it, meteors which shoot far away to die. *Quia pulvis es, et in pulverem reverteris,* with a pinch of ash on the hair.

I imagine the young Horatio around the world, Shakespeare escaped from Stratford-upon-Avon, from his wife, his children, from the dearest affections, free to exist, always making existence difficult after complex situations, instead of enjoying the simple things life has in store for us. Horatio might not be like the people who aspire to change your life, to save you from evil and lead you towards good. *It is your soul I buy from you, I withdraw it from black thoughts ... and I give it to God.* Still, I look up to him as a person who can help you find beams of light, spend serene moments that might momentarily let you enjoy life, discover a deeper sense. His life, our life, enriched with lots of common stories of far off things, ancient sorrows that have been, and may be again.

Horatio is quite intrigued with professor Brough's study on *Hamlet* by Shakespeare, and when I tell him he is a guest at Forrester Court Care Home, near Paddington, he promptly says to me:

'I know where it is.'

I imagine this good man walking about London, kilometers and kilometers, to run into disoriented people like me, and with everybody he searches for the reason why this immanent will keeps us active, full of projects, also when we are old, always with the hope we'll manage to leave something behind, maybe just a sign which makes us say I was, I did, I am important somehow, I haven't lived for nothing.

Horatio well explains to me we aren't far, and after a few steps along Hyde Park across Kensington Gardens you get to Queensway, where there are a lot of pleasant, little places to grab a snack cheaply. And at the bottom of the street, behind Paddington railway station, you get to the old people's home. This adventure intrigues him, above all thanks to Shakespeare, to hear from a professor something different about this great man. A study which isn't the gossip of newspapers which write ninety per cent of English people know just the titles of two of his works, or think he is contemporary, or he is gay, a member of the beat generation or other nonsense which prove that idiots' mother is always pregnant, that ignorance is strength … touch it and the bloom is gone.

It's half past seven in the morning with already lots of people around. The great metropolis is in the excitement of the rush-hour. London is special on a beautiful morning of summer sunshine. A medley of people who walk fast down Queensway, a cosmopolitan street, loads of restaurants, oriental above all, cafes and small shops, Pakistani, Indian, supermarkets 24/7. The lady at the till and her husband at the exit to check that customers don't run away without paying. Things are cheap, they don't want to take advantage. Those people are in transit after all, who will see them any more? And their community grows, develops, always ready to give a hand to one another. A world of sacrifices we, Friulians, have long forgotten. We do not understand any more, where those Christians, Muslims, or who else, find a goal, an objective, an aim in life to go ahead, happy of what they manage to put together day by day, happy to be in this world, to be an example of honesty. A great teaching to their children who grow protected in a family with important values. Money, wealth give to you with one hand and take it with the other, and you feel poor inside.

BREAKFAST AT AN ENGLISH CAFE

Horatio walks confidently. You can see he knows the area like the back of his hand. He enters an unpretentious, family-run cafe. He says hello to the hostess, an English lady in her sixties with an unkempt, dull appearance, used to the same customers for years, with the same traditional dishes, easy to please. The curtains of the large window on the outside knew queen Victoria. A smell of frying spreads throughout the whole space, and an almost natural filth, deposited dirt, of worn out and old things settles on the whole place.

The owner has got two owl eyes, a harsh stare, the expression Carnian people have when they see a stranger. What did you come to do up here, to pester us? It makes me think Horatio might have a bad reputation regarding paying. The lady looks at me with suspicion. The same sort, no work, no money and no food. If they eat without paying, they'll have to deal with my husband, who surely won't make them do the washing up, but will call the bobby.

The place is small, five tables with the top in laminated plastic, without a tablecloth, with unpretentious chairs. Just two of us. We don't have time to sit down that the owner hands a plastic card to us with the breakfast menu written on one side and the lunch menu on the other side. Luckily, all the dishes are cheap, a trouble less. Now, we'll have to see who's going to pay for Horatio. If he charges me the service of accompanying me around London, I'm duped. The most convenient dish is the English breakfast: a crust of bacon, a scrambled egg and a squirt of beans in a tomato sauce with a glass of milk. I might get by with this food for the whole week. Two meals at five pounds for the next five days makes fifty quid. Not bad, even though afterwards they should pump out my stomach or give me an anema. I remember my grandma used to knead the polenta in her fist and dip it in the lard. Never fed. Half polenta board just for herself, old days' hunger, dire poverty, to scrape the pot. At old people's feast, around Christmas, she happily walked around with slices of mortadella coming out of her coat pockets. They might come in useful, you can't rule hunger, you don't know about tomorrow, or at dinner. Let's love one another is written on the Caritas van. Let's open the Charity door at Saint Peter's Cathedral, and close the Mercy door. Watch out drafts to open so many doors. Watch out the wind under the door! You'll see, you'll see, poverty will be back! You've got used to squandering like a sponger. Use money frugally, put it aside, save it, you don't know the future. The dog always digs up the bone underground, that's a friend to man.

Horatio looks at me while he is soaking a piece of bread into the beans sauce.

'I wonder if you are enjoying breakfast,' he asks me.

Sure, to smack my lips. Each country with its own cuisine. But how different Sauris spek is, and the omelet with new-laid eggs and hops! And what do Carnian beans have in common with tinned Heinz Beans? Nothing.

The owner comes to us, just a bit more opened up, when we are about to pay. She isn't an ugly woman, a little British, a little stiff on two rather wooden legs.

'Enjoyed breakfast?' she inquires.

Again!? It took me fifteen years to get used to pumpkin *zuf,* the Friulian intestinal regulator. So hot to get your tongue burnt the first morning, then the next day, two days after that and on, with hot milk to form a sort of mush. Quite a different thing from bifidus actiregularis, with the gorgeous women of commercials who are so light and wiggle their hips like butterflies!

Horatio is really happy. Proteins in the morning. On Sundays a good broth with the oldest chicken in the roost. Fat blotches moving about like boats in the bowl, after boiling for hours in the pot during the Mass, and for the second course to pick the meat from the hen's leg, the best food. It's hard to run after a ball, third amateur division, worn out and with the intestine which rumbles. 'What are you doing back there in the defense?' The exhaustion which doesn't let me run in the mud and I also have to be scolded by the coach on a rainy Sunday in my teens. 'Why does the coach put that poor youth in the team? He can hardly stand!' And afterwards you cry at home, because you are not like the others, you lack something, and the simple-minded company that annoys me. 'He isn't gay, is he?' I could hardly sing that skanky song, so dirty, I felt ashamed. After every victory, the coach started in his bass voice. 'And the cunt without hairs, and the cunt without hairs looks like a sore. And the dick turned inside out, and the dick turned inside out, a road assassin.' And then everybody after him. Once, twice and so on. 'And fill the glass of that poor boy to wet his whistle!'

The bell-tower clock of Heaven Church nearby strikes eight. It's time to settle the bill. Out of politeness it would be my duty to pay, still, when you are short of money, to pull out the wallet is a great distress. Sharing Dutch would be the best solution, also because we've spent more or less the same amount, but Horatio offered to be my guide, and often friendship gets stronger with an act of generosity.

Come on Guglielmo, be brave, that the sun eats up the

hours!

A moment of fatal distraction. Horatio is speaking to the lady. You can see they are in close terms and, as it happens in similar circumstances, they bring the conversation round to the news, to the little man, to the stranger I am.

'He is Italian, here in London on a mission …' Horatio says to her.

'Yes, yes … for important matters.' What am I going to tell the lady here now?

'Yes, yes, an important meeting with a professor who taught in Italy for many years.'

And since she's placed me in the category of very important people, I add that I am from near Venice.

'Oh yes, Venice, Saint Mark's Basilica, the Doge's Palace, the Bridge of Sighs, the gondola … been there three times. How lucky you are!'

Not really Venice, almost an hour and a half by car and two hours to find parking, three hours on the local train which stops at every dog's piss.

Horatio might have gone to the bathroom. I can't see him. I hope he won't let me alone with the owner and the romance of her life, the exchange of the engagement ring with her betrothed in a gondola on the Grand Canal, and the glittering of the moon on the silvery water on a hot August night. Hand on my wallet, we are Friulians, we suffered from poverty and spending has always been a sensitive spot not to mention. With great distress, let's produce the pounds the Committee for Friulian Hamlet gave to me with kind generosity.

Twist in the tale.

'It's okay. Horatio paid,' she says to me with a sardonic smile.

A murky feeling overwhelms me, a mix of sensations,

divided between the incapability of reinforcing the friendship with Horatio with a noble act of generosity, and an instinctive, coward, but also pleasant sensation I didn't draw on my little capital brought along from Friuli.

It was quite obvious that it was my turn to pay, since Horatio offered to accompany me to destination. I always feel a sensation of hanger to myself, of annoyance, when things don't go as I'd have liked them to go, as I'd imagined them, and I am always ready to get mad for the umpteenth example of indecision.

Here he is, coming back from the bathroom. Never neglect the little things of life.

'Horace, thank you for breakfast,' I say to him, and then I express my slightly pretended malcontent.

'You shouldn't have … I was supposed to pay!'

Ignoble refrain. It was my turn, it was your turn. He is my guide in London, he also pays my breakfast, and I can neither reciprocate here now, because another egg with fried bacon would send me knock out. A cup of hot water with a vague taste of coffee might be the solution to pay him back right away.

'No, that's okay. Next time!' Horatio replies without a shadow of doubt.

Who knows what is for me to pay next time. I'll have to economize on food if I want to get to the end of the week. I don't want to rummage about in the rubbish. A glass of milk is almost free. It might be enough in the morning, and before going to bed in order to get to sleep.

We say goodbye to the owner, who is now in confidence. Venice has opened her heart in an epiphany of sounds, colors and perfumes. Spiritually, we Italians are used to beauty, to the art of our cities, to the enchantment of the landscape, and don't appreciate enough their value if foreigners don't remind us. Venice has eased the British aplomb of the lady.

THE MEETING WITH AMLÊT

The bell-tower clock of St Matthew's Church strikes nine, with a dead sound on the final stroke of nine. Together with Horatio we set out at a good pace down Queensway. We are in the middle of a crowd, a movement of people who elbow their way towards the center, the nearest tube station, the bus stop. A procession of people: dressed up clerks, women holding their handbags tight and wiggling their hips in the snug leggings, little streams which from side alleys flow into Queensway. Hurrying, hurrying, legs going quick quick quick in ignoble haste, for fear of being late. A multitude, I had not thought death had undone so many. Where are they going in such a hurry, at a brisk pace, tic-e-tac, towards the common fate?
I glance at a person standing in the middle of the throng. He is staring at something in front of him, but we don't know what he is watching and why. People pass him quickly on both sides, a river in flood, and he's stuck like a seagull, no reaction, no trouble, he is undecided where to go and what to do, a brother. He doesn't look like a new face, rather a fellow countryman, a Friulian abroad, even though it isn't likely to bump into acquaintances here in London, among anonymous people. He too has caught sight of me for a while, no time to check, to get a bit closer, to try to guess. An actor, a politician, a footballer or a twit whatsoever like me? There, transfixed, to see the world go round him. Horatio moves ahead with his purposeful stride. It is difficult to keep up with him. Still, I've got the sensation of being followed, that somebody is after us. Who is the third who always walks beside us? Is it a spirit who torments us, an obsession, a doubt, or a

good angel who shows us the way?

I spin round and I see him behind. A lanky young man, dirty, with long hair, an unshaven beard, a shabby shirt and jeans, a run-down chap, a poor soul.

'Amlêt! It's you, isn't it?' I stop him in a throng of people pushing me from behind.

'Amlêt! Tell me about you!' He gazes fixedly at me but he doesn't see me. He tries to understand where he is, to realize the dangerous situation he's got ahead. An expression of fear, of anxiety, of loneliness in this evil world full of people who judge, quarter, kill. The world has raised its whip; where will it descend? A pallid face, weary, annoyed, ruffled hair, used to eating what he finds in the street, sleeping where it comes. Amlêt! For how many days hasn't he heard his name, shared affection, experiences with somebody? He tries to focus on what is going on. Is it possible to chance on somebody from your same village in London, one of the few he would like to see, to meet, to speak to, to feel close? He glimpses Horatio, as if something strange and invisible to the so called normal was concentrated on my guide, the evil of the world, a world that burns, consumes. He himself alone, Amlêt, an obstacle, a rub, a bother, better to fade away forever. A person like him can't stay down here, in this bad world. No one will ever understand him, give him a hand, help him to return from the parallel world, the world of poets, prophets and the insane.

'Guildenstern! Rosencrantz!' Amlêt suddenly shouts at us, with people looking back at him.

'You two are looking for me, aren't you? Go away I don't want to see you!'

'No! It's me, Guglielmo from Camino. Don't you recognize me?'

'Away, away! Don't get closer! Don't touch me!' the poor chap shouts even louder, with his hands in front to protect himself.

'Tell me it's you, Amlêt, that I am not muddled, that a strange combination let us meet here in London. Is it possible?' I try to reassure him about my true intentions.

'I am not Amlêt you are looking for, Amlêt who passes for mad, the fool everybody teases, the idiot you pay a drink to, in order to laugh behind his back …'

'Oh, it's really you, from my own village!'

'Though people don't believe me, I am the last heir of the noble family of the marquis da Camino,' he says to me more quietly.

'All right. It doesn't matter whether you are Amlêt I know, or, as you tell me, Amlêt from the noble family of the marquis da Camino. The important fact is that we met here in London, in the middle of a multitude of people, impossible thing. Unbelievable! We two who come from a little village, from a little homeland. It must have been a sign of fate. It had to happen, that's all, it is destiny.'

'Don't come close to me! Don't look at me that way!' Amlêt says loud in a sort of delusion.

I know what he thinks of me, so dirty I am, with a long beard and long hair. A deviant, a person who hasn't been able to do anything in his life. I know I don't wash myself, I am repugnant. A fool who doesn't have a place to stay in this world, who can't have a family near him, a family that helps him. I have never wanted to relate to them, relatives, people from my village. I always fell out with my father. You are a good-for-nothing. At your age I knew what to do in my life. But I wasn't like him, I have never been and I don't want to be like him. I know, I see a different future is awaiting me. That's why I came to look for it here in

London. And after that I'll go as an outcast about the world. All of us are up to a different future. My father always humiliated me. You can't do it, we must be patient with you, very patient. Why going to school? It isn't for you. If you find a modest employment, apprenticed to somebody to learn a job, a small pay at the end of the month. We can't demand anything from someone like you. I saw him dangling like salami from a beam of the barn. I wasn't fourteen yet, and immediately I went to call granddad who pulling himself up the ladder came to see, and then he lay down, unable to stand, his hands on the face. He started weeping. He didn't want me to look at him and my heart was bursting out and feeling my stomach turn I couldn't breathe. And I didn't dare cast a side glance at that thing dangling, to see it every night before getting to sleep, suddenly during the day, an obsession, a torment I couldn't forget. 'A shame, a shame!' granddad kept repeating and didn't want to call anybody. 'What can people think? A shame!!' he continued repeating endlessly. I went down the ladder and got to cry behind the house, on the embankment. A man, who was working in the field nearby, saw me. 'What's going on, lad? Why are you crying?' Since then I started having hallucinations. I liked staying alone, not seeing anybody, just granddad and I. To overcome loneliness, I used to go to the granary or to the barn wearing a sort of greatcoat to become one of my heroes, an invincible myth. Fool, people from my village used to call me when I roamed alone down the embankment at dusk, and escaped from them. A wild young man who can't go off well in life. But I've never given a damn about people and I read, I studied till I found who I am truly. All of us are inside somebody who can't reveal himself.

'Amlêt, so you recognize me! You know who I am. Let me tell you how happy I am to see you.' I get closer in order to hug him, but Amlêt keeps me afar with his hand.

'Who's sending you to look for me here in London? Guildenstern, your gaze betrays you!'

'Come on Amlêt! Only chance made it possible for us to meet here in London. Nobody is sending me!'

'Rosencrantz, the man with you, sent you looking for me!'

'No, Amlêt! He is a Londoner, a nice person I met early this morning on a bench in Hyde Park. He offered to accompany me to a certain professor Brough. Wait here a moment, I'll inform him about you.'

I go to Horatio who stopped to wait for us a few steps further on.

'Do you mind Horatio? I met this guy from my same village. Incredible, isn't it?'

'Good. We can have a coffee with him. Shall we?' Horatio hints at a local nearby he knows well.

'He doesn't like company. I don't think he is going to stop with us,' I say to him.

Horatio realizes the situation is a bit complicated, and finds an excuse to give us the possibility to clear it up.

'Don't worry! I'll be waiting for you. Okay?'

'Thank you, Horatio.'

'I'll have a look at the shop over there, and back in a few minutes.'

He crosses the street to enter an antique shop.

Amlêt and I move a bit aside from the passage to better understand the incredible circumstance which made us meet in the center of London.

'Amlêt, tell me something about you. What are you doing here in London? Are you working?'

'Always with questions! All the same! Where are you

going, what are you doing, everybody belches out.'
'I just wanted to convey my surprise, the pleasure of
seeing you in a moment I didn't expect …'
'Man delights not me,' Amlêt suddenly says to me getting
some reminiscences out of his reading.
'I see the lessons I gave to you on Shakespeare have been
of use. You might be ready for a recital,' I say to him with
a bit of irony.
'No recital! It's the story of my life, the story of prince
Amlêt.'
'Sorry, I was joking,' I say to him trying not to offend him.
'I am the true Amlêt, just me, the last son of the cursed
family of the da Camino. Here is the silver ring I always
have with me, the blazon of the marquis da Camino.'
'I believe you, but still everything seems so strange. This
meeting of ours was predestined. Fate made us meet.
Amlêt, you too have to do with my visit to London.'
'As I thought at once. They sent you to look for me and
close me in a mental hospital.'
'No, wait that I'll tell you …'
'Just a few months, they promise. For your own good …
You take these tablets for your nerves and you'll soon feel
better. And then other tablets, always better than those you
were taking before, till you don't know where you are and
what they are doing to you. Your hands shake … we are
going to do something to your brain …'
'None of this. I swear, Amlêt. I swear! Listen to me that
I'll tell you the news. Your belief, which drove you here to
London, is that you are a noble, the last heir of the extinct
family of da Camino from Treviso, isn't it?'
'I'm feeling it inside. A voice keeps saying it to me. You'll
have to overcome the fear of fear, the fear of doubt, of the
diffidence of common people who poison your blood. You

belong to noble people. You are called to do great things, born with the caul. Pick up the plant of fennel and beat the ziringè …'

'Leave all these things now. I was about to tell you that also Shakespeare might have known about the marquis da Camino, at least according to the opinion of a famous medievalist, a certain professor Brough.'

Amlêt isn't surprised at all, and now seems to follow me, and for the moment to have forgotten the suspicion, the fear, of ending up sectioned in a madhouse.

'Shakespeare has always been my obsession,' he says to me. 'I dream about him at night. I've learned the whole tragedy *Hamlet* by heart to try to get in touch with him. I must go to Stratford-upon-Avon on his tomb to feel his closeness, to communicate with him. I've got so many things to ask him …'

'One day we can go together,' I say to him in order to win his diffidence.

'All right, but I must go now. I don't want that man to take me to his psychiatric clinic. They are looking for me everywhere, but they won't find me so easily.'

'Who? Horatio? He is a retired English teacher. When he comes back, we'll go straight to this professor Brough who, as I was about to tell you, believes, he is convinced that Shakespeare drew inspiration from the nobles da Camino to write the tragedy *Hamlet*.'

'*Hamlet* by Shakespeare?' Amlêt inquires astonished, more and more involved in the story. 'He pretended he was mad to find out the truth about his father's death,' he says. 'Instead, I do it to forget my father's suicide.'

'I didn't want to tell you, but you look saner than lots of characters who go about freely. Yours seems to me a recital, there is method in your madness. And I see a lot of coincidences which make this matter more than a historic research a sort of ghost-busting in the distant past. According to this professor, *Hamlet* by Shakespeare might be linked to the history of your ancestors, and precisely to Rizzardo the Second da Camino, who most likely was assassinated by his brother Guecellone on the fifth of April thirteen twelve.'

'I must look for a contact with Shakespeare and try to understand the things he knew I don't know about my past yet. I must go to Stratford on his tomb. I perceive I am near the truth.'

'You might be, but I suggest first you should come with us to professor Brough, who surely must have found out something else about the case of Friulian *Hamlet*.'

Now the young man is attentively following my discourse, and I can't help but be a bit funny, maybe for tiredness or for the exhaustion growing inside me.

'Who knows how happy the president of the Committee for Friulian Hamlet might be if he finds out that Amlêt, the old miller's grandson, isn't mad, off his head, but the link which could connect Shakespeare with the Trevisan marquis. Camino al Tagliamento might twin with the Danish town of Helsingør where the tragedy is set, and become a world center of Shakespearean studies.'

After a while seeing the youth rather thoughtful about such unexpected events, I add with a jeering smile:

'Amlêt, they might celebrate you on a procession with the brass band!'

'I know you all very well! You want to close me up with your stupid flattery!' Amlêt answers back rather irritated.

'I am so sorry. I'm feeling mortified. Everything happening to me seems so absurd, and has driven me insane.'

Guglielmo is a nice person. He's always cherished me. Now he invites me to go to this professor with him and Rosencrantz, who doesn't look like the shrinks who treated me in the past. Do I have to accept? I shouldn't, still after so much roving, you feel the need, the warmth of exchanging a few words with someone. A friendly hello felt in the heart, or also just listen to the sound of your language in a foreign country, a sensation which runs down your back, kindles a light inside you.

'All right. I'm coming to the professor with you, but without that Rosencrantz who is after me.'

'Horatio? We can't. He knows the way and is a nice person. He can help you as well if you really want to stay in London, when I return to Friuli.'

'Okay, but why won't you stay in London?' he asks me with affection.

'No, I must return. I don't have money to stay here, and my family is waiting for me in Friuli. I am not a rover like you, I don't feel like wandering around the world without the certainty of coming back to a safe harbor. The new, the different always frighten me, the gravity force attracts me towards a little world of affection and love, which I might never have enjoyed so far. And then I've already told you I'm here on this mission from the Committee which might be to my own advantage and to the territory as well if everything matches.'

'I'll never return to Camino. People even make me sick! For them I am the lunatic to close up in a madhouse. Better to live free, of illusions … here is Rosencrantz back, ready to take me with him.'

'Hi Horatio!' I go to him and explain the new situation. 'My countryman has agreed to come with us. Do you mind?'

'Not at all. He is welcomed,' he replies with the usual friendly nature which characterizes him.
Horatio, Hamlet and William. We have the playwright, the actors and we need the director. Professor Brough might produce our comedy. Or is it a tragedy? We'll see when we meet professor Brough. He'll decide. We are almost there.

THE VISIT TO FORRESTER COURT

Forrester Court Care Home is a two-story building, Victorian style, in a quiet area of London, busy with passers-by to Paddington railway station or to the offices of London administration. It is neither a residential nor a tourist area. A small gate with three steps and a short passage bordered with roses leads us to the entrance.
A nurse comes towards us.
'Morning. How can I help you?'
'Good morning. We'd like to speak to professor Brough,' I explain to her the reason of our visit.
'Sorry. Did you say professor …?'
'Professor Brough. B.R.O.U.G.H.' I spell the letters of his surname.
'There isn't a professor that I know here.'
'I'm sure he is here. Could you kindly check the computer?' I ask her cordially.
'Maybe, he hasn't been here long. I'll go and check.'
'Thank you.'
Now it comes out that professor Brough isn't here, or even worse that the professor doesn't exist, has never existed, or as it occurs in Shakespeare's comedies, it's just an exchange of identity, or a dream. *And this weak and idle theme, no more yielding but a dream'.*
Here she is. The nurse is back with an amused, hardly comforting smile which is more revealing than words.
'I am so sorry!' she says. 'Yes, Mister Brough. We are so used to calling him the poet that we've almost forgotten his true name! He always keeps mumbling by himself to someone he calls Sheikh Spear It sounds like that. He must be an Arab, I suppose.'

Here it is, one of the great experts on Shakespeare mumbles in Arabic. The demolition of the character has already begun. Professor Brough who raves alone with a sheikh from Dubai. Where has all his history passed at universities gone, the respectful silence, the devotional attention at the conventions in half of Europe. Vanitas, vanitatum. To strut and fret an hour upon the stage and then is heard no more. Myths crumble, categories are canceled out in the relentless progress of time. The almost devotional respect towards authority something of the past. I remember the priest in my village was an important figure, he had everybody's respect. *'Praised be Jesus Christ,'* I said to the new priest when I was little. He looked at me with wonder, as about to say: 'Where have I got?' He sent me away with *'Mandi'*, and I, a little boy, remained there, astonished, waiting for that reassuring *'Forever and Ever'* which has never come since then. Beliefs gone to the dogs, faith which dwindles, all the same, we are trying to give our life a meaning before disappearing forever and ever. It makes me think of those great personalities, great teachers I've known in the schools of half Friuli, during my temporary teaching jobs. They gave themselves great importance when they spoke in the meetings. Now nobody knows anything about them. Professor What's-its-Name isn't worth a brass farthing, his loquacity was a meteor, not even the Assembly Hall walls have memory of him. I can't remember their names any more. Plunged into abyss. Nothing any more. Why do we have to create so many illusions of greatness, if afterwards all of us end up in forgetfulness? Men's words are limited because he is limited in time and space. Nothing stands but for time's scythe to mow.
'Would you mind awaiting the professor in the lounge?'

the nurse says to us.

'I'll take him there if he is awake in his room.'

'Yes, sure.'

'Please, I recommend you should speak to him slowly and clearly, you shouldn't rise the tone of your voice or get angry,' she adds in a professional attitude. 'You know, he suffers from senile dementia.'

'Okay. Thank you.'

The nurse quickly leaves the entrance and disappears down the corridor to the bedrooms.

'Christ have mercy on us!' the situation makes me think at once.

We sit down on an old sofa in the lounge waiting for the professor. With folded arms we weigh the pros and cons. The modest building which hosts him, the ignorant nurse who takes care of him, and how she presented him, the poet who talks by himself with a certain Sheikh Spear, makes me think professor Brough is an old man over eighty, ill and with a disturbed mind.

Gazing fixedly at the patch of blue sky outside the window, as in hospital to withdraw the tests with the numbers which move slowly, one step to the final judgment, and the wish of being outside in the mountains, where it seems you can touch the sky. In those moments up there in Carnia, you can even think the world isn't just chaos, but there is a project, a precise design, and the perfection of the universe isn't just a law of physics, but the creation of a superior mind, and for a moment you think you cherish everybody, forgive enemies, begin another life and you are eternal. Christ have mercy on us!

Horatio seems amused and lives the situation with expectation, with the pragmatic spirit of English people, while I live the meeting with anxiety and the fear of the certain failure. Amlêt, lost in his world, seems he is taken in his sick fantasies. A light fissure from the window which illuminates an unknown world, a noise, a strong dissonance, hands on his ears to stop that violence, Munch's Scream, shocks of energy in a sick brain. Living in a parallel world, in a dreamed reality, the world of artists, day-dreamers, lunatics and all of us who haven't stopped believing. We are such stuff as dreams are made on; and our little life is rounded with a sleep.

You can hear a few steps dragged on the floor and a continuous muttering.

'No, no, no! Let me alone! … I can walk myself! Go! I don't want to see anybody!' professor Brough expresses his discontent.

'Don't bother, poet! They are friends. They want to speak to you,' the nurse tries to reassure him.

'Oh, don't call me poet! Far from the madding crowd! Far, far from this sick world!' he shouts.

Professor Brough jerks forward leaning on a cane, controlled by the nurse. He is a hunchbacked small man, around eighty years of age, gray and ruffled hair, wisps of beard growing here and there on a furrowed face. The fixed gaze reveals he can't see well, and can't recognize the people in front of him. The nurse tries to accompany him, but the professor, quite irritated, shoves her away with one hand.

'I am sick when I do look on you!' he shouts at her.

'Quiet, quiet, old man!'

You can easily understand that professor Brough was forced to come here, against his will. Similar situations often occur, where he cares about his autonomy, even though he sees his body doesn't obey the brain commands any more, and it doesn't give the correct support. The poor man realizes he isn't himself any more, he doesn't have the control of what he is doing, and sees the real world fade away with all the people who adorn it. Everything is confused, the impossibility of organizing the present, and flashes from the past, fragments of memories that suddenly come out like sparks which kindle and die. Double fit of anger, against those who help him and against himself, against the world and the damned fate of getting old and die.

The nurse accompanies him to sit down in front of us. Quite a hard effort, made of movements forward and backward till recoiling and flopping on to the armchair.

'Good morning, professor Brough,' I greet him nicely.

'Morning,' he mutters with a rather resigned attitude, little used to be in company. But it's just a moment, because his manner gets friendlier, even curious.

'Methinks I should know you, and know these two people. Yet, I am doubtful, for I am mainly ignorant... Italians, aren't you?'

'Yes, we two are Italians.'

'What's your name?'

'Guglielmo is my name, and my two friends are Horatio and Amlêt.'

'Your name's William in English, isn't it? Like William Shakespeare! The Bard. Are you the one who came here yesterday?'

'Oh no. Not me. This time yesterday I was still in Friuli.'

'I was told someone would come today or tomorrow... Italians, they said … Who said so? They've taken away all my things. I don't have a pen to write any more, to report my thoughts, my ideas, so that I can remember! My memory is getting worse … time after time … I can't see my memory improve. Not any more.'

'Don't say it professor Brough! Who knows what tomorrow may bring,' Horatio comforts him. 'Never lose hope!'
Tomorrow, and tomorrow, and tomorrow, from day to day … You know William Shakespeare, the poet, don't you?'
'Yes, oh yes … Macbeth, act five, scene five,' Horatio shows interest, but I start losing hope because of the professor's absurd speaking.
'Professor Brough, Shakespeare fits perfectly, but I'd like you to tell me something about *Hamlet.*' I try to explore what recollections the professor has of the tragedy *Hamlet.*
'You're Shakespeare lovers!... You're poets!...He's sent you here!' he thinks we are on a mission on behalf of the great English poet.
'Oh no, professor Brough. We are not sent by Shakespeare,' I reply rather resigned.
'I am here with these two friends of mine on a mission about the sources of *Hamlet.*' I try to explain to him the real reason of our visit, but I am soon interrupted.
'Friends, friends … we all need somebody to love on the way to *an undiscovered country...*' quoted the professor.
'… *From whose bourn no traveler returns.*' I complete the quotation from *Hamlet* thinking more about the impossible coming round of the disturbed human mind than the impossible coming back after death of the famous monologue, *'To be or not to be'.*
'You quoted Shakespeare! You too are a poet … let me think... The teacher friend I had in Vicenza looked like you, the same bewildered expression in his eyes. I asked him once if he felt good, if he was happy. He told me he had a wife, children, a beautiful house … which surprised me. He must have had something … with the bewildered expression he had... It happens when you least expect it.

Between the age of forty and fifty. Critical age ... you start feeling about your failures ... I taught at Vicenza University. Do you know Vicenza?'

'We are from Udine, near Vicenza.'

'Can you spell that name?'

'U-D-I-N-E.'

'Yes, I know the place, but I can't remember where I heard about it. My memory is no good ... pray, don't mock me. I am a very foolish fond old man ... I don't know where I am now. Is this a brothel I am in? And what am I doing here? Even though you tell me now who you are and what you want ... two minutes and everything's gone. Forgotten, deleted ... Sorry, my mind doesn't work so well ... Hideous puppet an aged man is. Decrepit. The rankest compound of villanous smell that ever offended nostril. Will I ever be able to get better? I've lost my hope.'

I look with compassion at the poor, old professor. In his eyes a great sorrow to see himself in that condition. He has surely had his part of glory in his life. Honors which brought him fame and fortune and everything that goes with it. It seems now, but everything was already written when we were born that if we are lucky to live longer, let's call it luck, we all will have to pass through that state, humble and overbearing, poor and rich. Sure, it helps whether a person has the possibility of remaining in his environment, whether he can maintain some points of reference with his past. However, this is less and less possible. Anyway, I'll have to make an attempt to see whether the myth of Friulian *Hamlet* is an invention of the net, fake news as people pass it off nowadays.

'Mister Brough, you surely remember what professor Clough, your collaborator and friend, found out about *Romeo and Juliet* in Udine,' I hint at professor Clough's research.

'What did he find out? I can't remember now,' he inquires with his eyes staring at me without expression.

'Professor Clough wrote that the tragedy *Romeo and Juliet* has nothing to do with the city of Verona, because the Capulets and the Montagues ...'

'*A plague on both your houses!* Yes, yes. The true story isn't from Verona, but from a city nearby.'

'Udine.'

'Oh yes, Udine ... let me think ... where is it exactly? Which way from here? Italy, isn't it? Paddington, West End and then, do I have to turn left or right? Oh yes, on the south bank of the river Thames, it must be near the Globe, I suppose ...'

Yes, across the river Thames, the Tagliamento ... it's a completely different world, foreign and unknown, in the mind of this poor man, lost in the quiet of a great past. His memory is like halos which kindle here and there and glimmer in the dark of a sick mind. A luminous halo surrounding us from the beginning to the end. Flashes of recollections, fragments of stories put together. Italy, England, Friuli ... a complete mess. Poor old man, poor all of us!

'But who are you and the two people here?' he asks me again. 'You told me before, didn't you? Oh! What I am now my sweetest friend, everything I know goes away in the end. I don't know anybody. Who said Guglielmo? The Conqueror? You were not with me at Hastings, were you?'

I, Guglielmo the Conqueror? The only thing I could conquer with difficulty was the piece of paper with 'Doctor' written on it, as for the rest, both work and family have been a surrender more than a conquest. Senile dementia. Bad thing. Fragments of thoughts which run after one another, the ball which spins quickly on the roulette wheel and lands on a number to form new combinations, a new vision of the world, where space and time do not exist any more, today and yesterday are the same, the living and the dead are together and speak to one another, hatred and love towards people agree before and after the meals, before going to bed or after waking up, circuits which touch or detach in the brain, turn on a light, flash a glimmer on a juvenile passion, suddenly matches it with a suffered wrong and the hatred to the person who did it. And everything turns to hate: of the present state, of the person nearby who takes care of you, of the whole world. *Away, you starvelling, you elf-skin, you dried neat's-tongue, bull's-pizzle, you stock-fish!*

Also this mission of mine in London might come to an end here, but why not try to come up with something positive even from the most hopeless cases. Amlêt is smiling and we realize he feels good with us. He's got company and the professor's jabbering intrigues him, urges him to find out the strand of the entangled ball of yarn of his monologues. He might be able to find a meaning in his delirium.

In truth, Amlêt is concentrated on the glimmer of light which filters through the curtain to end its course on the professor's wrinkled hand on the sofa arm. In the light, it looks like the hand of Pope Innocent X in Bacon's picture, with the blue veins protruding on his smooth skin, turquoise branches of the Tagliamento river in the dazzling gravel of the Friulian piedmont.

It is strange that after roving so much around London, alone, trying to procure food in the bins and sleep where it comes, I am here together with people who call me by name … Amlêt … It's beautiful to hear your name after so long. People who listen to you, don't send you away, actually, they make you part of their life. And this old man here, I understand him well, suspended in a world just his own, without rules and thousands of trifles which nag the existence in today's sick world. The professor's ancient hand on the sofa arm, the Methuselah body, the intelligence of a prophet, by chance has he ever been to see something from the afterlife? Who am I? Amlêt, really? What is my destiny and what would it have been if I had been born rich or in another family, in another country? And if I hadn't been born, who would have taken my place?

All the people who laugh at me, make fun of me, pay for my drinks to see me play the fool, as loading the spring of a puppet to see it dance a moment, what do those people know about themselves, about what they are doing, where they are going, or are they like a rolling stone which plunges into the void of their existence? How does it feel to be a complete unknown? I'm sure that in my chemistry it is written a different destiny. I see myself like prince Hamlet who realizes he is destined for great enterprises, but he can't accept evil in the world, he can't get rid of the doubts which torment him. He destroys himself, his family, like the marquis da Camino, my ancestors, who end up by committing a fratricide and disappear from history soon after. The destiny of all men who lose their mind because of greed for power. *What is this quintessence of dust? Man delights not me.* I don't want to be like this … Mad, they call me, but can they see how they are inside, where they are going?

A COMPLICATED MATTER

A moment of fatigue, a moment of meditation, a sacred moment, to free yourself from the weight of your body and glide in a parallel life. Professor Brough's identity's fading out into a gray impalpable world. I give in to despair and look at the poor, old man, whose eyes are closing little by little, and some drool is coming out of his mouth and trickling down the chin.
Who are we? Where are we going? Who is watching our journey? The void? The instinct of the little ant which quickly runs to the anthill, or a Supreme Being, God? Abraham's God? *Has he a beard, Mister Godot? Fair or ... white?* Might the God master, with a white beard, as old as the hills, ever solve our doubts? I'm asking the sacrifice of your only son. You must kill him, sacrifice him to my glory. Are we off our head? Abraham, aged over one hundred, might likely have had a bit of Alzaheimer, but still, how can you kill your only child? Not even if there were ten, twelve of them: Primo, Secondo ... Firmino. What terrible God makes things turn out the way he wants! He is on our side. Guaranteed heaven if you kill the infidel. He is like you, the same as you, but he was born in the country nearby, the same sun, the same glee and suffering, but he was taught another language, another culture, another religion. We can't kill him for this, can we? And in percentage, what possibilities do we have to govern our destiny according to our wishes? Is it much better to be in the center of things, and then feel the vacuity even stronger, the chill of existence, when others abandon you and you get old and decrepit?
Mister Brough opens his eyes after a light daze. The effect

of the medication which calm him, numb him, but make him lose awareness of the real world, cancel that shred of memory that puts together relations among people.

He stares at me with a wry smile, happy to be still with the living.

'Who are you? Still here?' he asks me again.

'I am Guglielmo. You don't know me, but I know you! Professor at Vicenza University. Shakespeare's critic and appreciated scholar of English Renaissance...'

'Yes, yes, yes, but I'm trying to understand how you know me ... I love Italy, but I was in Vicenza last year ... or was it ten years ago? ... I can't remember. Yet, I am doubtful now, locked up in this home. I am mainly ignorant what place this is, and all the skills I have. I don't see anybody. I feel lonely, very lonely ... My salad days, have long passed away. When I was green in judgment, cold in blood, to do as I did then ... What have I done today? Nothing. What did I do yesterday? I can't remember ... It's a shadowy world, skies are slippery gray ... Oh, I feel like crying,' the professor ends the monologue with a self-pity lament.

'Mister Brough, in Italy it is believed that *Hamlet's* true story by Shakespeare occurred in the Trevisan March and not in Denmark,' I say to him, hardly convinced to kindle a light in the professor's distressed mind.

'Words, words, words ... Speak more clearly, young man!'

I forgot the nurse's recommendation to speak to him slowly and clearly.

'Professor, in Italy they think that *Hamlet*'s tragedy didn't occur at Elsinore Castle, in Denmark ...'

'You said Elsinore, you said about Prince Hamlet ... *the earth appears no other thing to me than a foul and pestilent congregation of vapors to me* ...' the professor interrupts me to make me understand with the quotation from *Hamlet* his thought about the human race.

He's guessed my belief without figuring out the real reason of my visit here in London. He tells us about a pestilent congregation of vapors, I'd use crap. There's always something that stinks. Sometimes some alchemy comes out by chance, by synaesthesia, and gives us the meaning of where we are and where we are going. Still, I'll have to find the reason why in Friuli they think that the source of *Hamlet* by Shakespeare is somehow linked to Rizzardo and Guecellone, marquis in Treviso, and to Camino al Tagliamento, soul place of the Trevisan noblemen.

'Professor Brough, you published a research at the university of Vicenza, *The Ordeal of the da Camino, marquis in Treviso.'*

'Did I? Yes, now I remember.'

'Is your work on the Trevisan marquis somehow related to the facts narrated in the tragedy *Hamlet* by Shakespeare?'

'I don't know what you mean, young man, still there are more things in heaven and earth than are dreamed of in our philosophy.' He hasn't understood my question well, still with the quotation from *Hamlet*, he explains his belief in how limited and partial human knowledge is, because man himself is limited, in time and space.

'Professor, didn't you speculate in your study that the events narrated in *Hamlet* might have happened in Italy, and refer to the supposed fratricide of Rizzardo the Second da Camino?'

'Tyrannical family, indeed! *There's ne'er a villain dwelling in all* Italy, *but he's an arrant knave.'* We might be on the right track. The professor remembered his study on the da Camino, and in the sentence from *Hamlet* he mistook Italy for Denmark. Is it just a Freudian lapsus, or when one thinks of thieves and delinquents, he immediately thinks of poor Italy? Still, it is worth while insisting to see whether something else comes out.

I don't think that the president, with the whole Committee for Friulian Hamlet, deliberately invented everything. A historian must have found that in the Middle Ages it doesn't come out that a Danish king or a nobleman killed his brother to seize power and marry his wife. A situation that might have happened in the Trevisan March. There's also the possibility that the professor or somebody else might have cited the Trevisan noblemen as an example to show the depravity of power at that time.

'Mister Brough, do you think that the sentence by Marcellus in *Hamlet*, *'something is rotten in the state of Denmark'*, is a generic sentence which might surely have gone well also for Italy, for England, and for the institutional and moral rot of the whole world at that time?'

'Yes, yes … To be honest, as this world goes, is to be one man picked out of ten thousand,' said professor Brough with a good clarity of mind.

Surely we needn't disturb Shakespeare, we needn't a ghost come out of a tomb to tell us that this world appears no other thing than a foul and pestilent congregation of vapors.

Even though the situation is quite clarified, I'll try to see whether from his work, *'The Ordeal of the da Camino'*, something interesting comes out for our president. Just in case he wants back the money of my journey to London.

'Professor, besides the suspicion that the marquis Rizzardo the Second might have been murdered by his brother Guecellone, there is also the possibility that a beautiful woman, Giovannina Visconti, married to Rizzardo, might have been involved in the murder.' I try to infer some historical events from his publication in order to spark his interest.

'We don't know. She was his second wife. A woman from an important Pisan family, praised by Dante Alighieri.'

'In your essay you also wrote that Dante Alighieri, in Paradise, Canto IX, tells us about Rizzardo's murder, didn't you?'

'Yes, yes … *carpir si fa la ragna* … As if to say that Rizzardo expected it. He was going with his head held high, but didn't know who was plotting against him. He was playing chess in his palace, when a villein hit his head with a hatchet.'

'With a hatchet!' Surely Shakespeare couldn't use such a peasant tool to murder a king. Instilling poison into one ear is certainly more regal.

'Professor Brough, might there have been Guecellone's complicity in the homicide?' I helplessly try to restate the theory which brought me to London.

'Who knows? … the guards killed the assassin. Maybe they wanted to hide something. Who can say it?' he confirms the possible fratricide.

'E dove Sile e Cagnan s'accompagna, tal signoreggia e va con la testa alta, che già per lui carpir si fa la ragna,' the professor quotes by heart. 'You told me you are a teacher, didn't you? This is a quotation from Dante Alighieri! You should know it!'

I realize that this is the end, that mister Brough has lost his patience, and that any moment he might enter his parallel world made of slumber and sudden outbursts of rage and malcontent. All the same I try to come to a conclusion with him.

'Professor, you confirm that the end of Rizzardo is the result of a political quarrel, and not a plot inside the

Trevisan family da Camino. And Shakespeare's *Hamlet* has nothing to do with this matter,' I ask him rhetorically.

'Tradition has a simultaneous existence and composes a simultaneous order,' the professor quotes, quite inspired. *'The present and the past exist simultaneously.* What's happening now here has already happened somewhere in the past. Who said that?' He stares at us, suddenly disoriented, waiting for the answer which doesn't come. After that he goes on like a river in flood towards the final drift.

'There's a lot we don't know about Shakespeare. Why did he abandon Stratford and his wife, Anne Hathaway ... He was forced to marry her, eight years older and with a baby in her womb ... She lived longer though. Women are more resilient. This was Lady Hathaway's revenge for his life as an artist away from home ... Critics say he died on his fifty-second birthday. He might have died during his birthday party. He was the actor of himself, the poor player that struts and frets his hour upon the stage ... And what about the dark lady in the sonnets? Was she a married woman or an alluring young lass? Oh, I am fed up of staying here! I must go now. You Italians, adieu, adieu, wonderful people, mandolin and cuisine ... Yes, yes. I must go home. This is not my place. Where is home? Right or left? I want to see my twin son, Hamnet! Where is my son? Hamnet, why is he running away from me? Stop him! Stop him ...!'

The professor tries to stand up with difficulty. He can't do it on his own, and the nurse, who has always been sitting nearby, hurries in his help.

'Don't touch me! I must go home! Don't touch me!' the professor shouts at her.

Also Horatio and I stand up in order not to be involved in

the quarrel between the nurse and professor Brough.
Everybody watches the scene quite desolate.
'This is no country for old men. An aged man is but a paltry thing, a terrible thing!' Horatio says to himself, without being heard by professor Brough. Meanwhile the professor continues his personal dispute with the nurse who tries to convince him to sit down with us again, but she ends up by irritating him even more.
'Away, go away. I wish you were clean enough to spit upon!' he shouts at her.
In this terrible situation I am the most exposed, the most humiliated by such unexpected events. I am looking for Horatio's comfort who understands the situation, comes to me and with his vicinity he tries to put heart into me, so, instinctively. He didn't understand a lot of passages of the conversation between professor Brough and me very well. They were quite obscure. He's been the spectator of a recital, an extract of the theater of the absurd, where the audience doesn't know whether to laugh or cry because of the characters' ridiculous, grotesque behavior. At the end everybody is disoriented. It is as if they've seen inside them the mirror of their fate, and live a sense of anxiety, of fear, of ridicule. Horatio didn't know anything of that story, of the da Camino, of Rizzardo the Second and his brother Guecellone, but he understood the importance those distant facts had for me, and how central the professor was in my expectations. He sees mister Brough dragging himself along, always chasing the nurse away with one hand. She tries to support him because he is staggering, quite insecure on his legs. This fact irritates him even more. He doesn't accept her help. He wants to do it by himself.
'You, stupid woman! The rankest compound of villanous

smell that ever offended nostril. I want to go home. This is not my place. Home is over there near the river Themes. Away, you fool! I'd beat you but I would infect my hands.'
The nurse tries to soothe him with sweet words:
'Come on! Be nice! I know you are a good man.'
With the physical strength of her thirty years of age, she succeeds in linking arms with him and accompanying him in small steps towards the door. Now professor Brough is looking at her completely disoriented. He doesn't know where he is and what he is doing. He is as come out of a bad dream, and obedient like a small foal he totters next to her. He nearly seems to be grateful he's entered the real world, as if confused by the experience he's lived in the moments of madness.

THE END OF A DREAM

I have helplessly been looking at the whole scene, the professor's raving, his loss of consciousness, of contact with the real world.

'This is no country for old men,' Horatio keeps saying with dejection and frustration looking at the professor dragging himself to the door. 'An aged man is but a tattered coat upon a stick,' he repeats in a litany. I shake my head at Horatio's bitter remark, while the professor has got to the door and leaves the scene. I can't do anything. Another dream which breaks down, a shooting star which falls away. There is nothing to hope. *An aged man is but a paltry thing, a tattered coat upon a stick, unless soul clap its hands and sing, and louder sing for every tatter in its mortal dress.*

It's useless, all useless. I believed in the president's invention, maybe influenced by the figure of Amlêt, either literary or real, by that young man disappeared from his village, a rover around the world.

Meanwhile, Amlêt is still sitting alone. He's put his hands on his ears not to listen to the shouting of the professor, 'this is not home, this is not my place,' as if seized with an inner delirium, gazing fixedly ahead, concentrated on a voice which shouts loud to look for a place where to hide himself, to escape from this wicked world which burns. It's better to put an end to this bad life. Lying on the ground, *with a thud, thud, thud in his brain, and then a suffocation of blackness.* And people think you are off your head. Tell me a word of comfort. I'd like to speak to my father, dangling like a bag beneath the beams of the barn. I couldn't explain to him my reasons. He didn't give me time to tell him it wasn't my fault if I didn't obey him, if I was no good at school. There is something that doesn't work in my brain. A continuous whisper, a murmur of voices which come from a distance. You must end it all. Enough! Enough!

I perceive Amlêt's distress.

'Amlêt, can you hear me? Is there anything I can do, give you a hand, do something for you?' I ask him.

I'm getting closer to comfort him like a father. I'm taking him by the hand, clasping it, and then with the other pulling him up from sitting, where he's stayed fixed, motionless, for the whole period. Amlêt, like a dead body who's entered a world of shadows where nobody loves him, nobody respects him.

'This professor here frightens me,' he says to me rather upset. 'He makes me think of my father's shadow I always dream about at night. He presents himself like Rizzardo da Camino, but I tell him you are not my father, I am the miller's son down the river banks. In the dream he keeps saying to me that his brother Guecellone killed him. And why might he have killed you? He was afraid of my illegitimate child, of you, Amlêt! But remember, remember … you are the only true heir. Here, I wake up in my bed, stunned, in a sweat.'

'Amlêt, this dream you've told me about is nothing but an invention of your anguished, disappointed, despondent mind, like mine now,' I say to him. 'You must come back to the real world, enough ghosts in your existence. You must appreciate the good in life, face events with a positive spirit. It won't be easy, but together we'll have to do our best, with courage and determination.'

Amlêt keeps staring at the door where the professor went out. Dazed in his thoughts, he seems not to have heard a word I told him. A lesson of optimism might not be a value I can pass on in this moment, with the despair of my nth failure which disheartens me.

Remained alone in the semi-darkness of the room, Horatio is the only person who can find a prompt solution, lead us out of the nursing home and see together whether everything is over with the professor, or there is hope left. I look at him in expectation of a signal, a reaction. Do we have to go out of here and where? Who knows whether it is still possible to speak to the professor once he's calmed down. Never despair till the end, *to the last syllable of recorded time*. Tomorrow he might clear up something on his publication about the marquis from Treviso. He might explain to us how in his opinion Shakespeare could have got to know the events of the nobles da Camino in order to write *Hamlet*, or deny every link and define the two facts completely isolated from each other. Not even so rare in the history of humanity since Cain up to the present day, the brother's murder for power, for a woman, for inheritance and so on.

'I think we must leave the nursing home now,' Horatio says to me in a low voice.

I look at him quite dejected, unable to provide a solution.

'I suggest going to my place, where I work and where I am offered a place to stay,' he says to me. 'We might have lunch there.'

'Oh, thank you. I'm very grateful!'

After having heartily accepted Horatio's invitation, my first thought is for Amlêt.

'He invites us for lunch where he works. Amlêt, are you coming too?' I ask him.

Amlêt can't hear. He can't understand me in that moment of distress.

'Sure you are coming with us!' I comfort him.

'Phoenix Hostel is the place. It is not that far,' Horatio explains to us.

'Horatio, we do commend us to you. Right now, my friend here and I are unable to decide anything.'

We are moving out of the nursing home in a silence that kills. Nobody to say goodbye, nobody to thank, nobody to ask whether it is still possible to see the professor again, with the staff reduced to the minimum because of the crisis.

Horatio is used to walking around London. He rarely takes a bus or a train.

'We'll walk there. Right? Can you?' He inquires.

'Yes, that's fine. Thank you.'

'I like walking,' Horatio explains. 'My God is the God of walkers. If you walk hard enough, you probably don't need any other God.'

What is better than wandering around London, around big cities? You feel free, you stop to look and think, and not only your body, but also your spirit is happy.

There must be something in our brain which urges us to walk down the roads of the world. The curiosity to look elsewhere for a different world, more beautiful, more honest, and the experience of walking is full of expectations, it is part of the dream world and we don't feel tired, our legs move freely and the point of arrival is just an intermediate stage of our final journey. Our way goes straight towards the desired destination, the enchanted mountain, Shangri-La, the island of our imagination, the utopia of our most hidden wishes, the idea to get to an ideal place where to stop in order to create something and leave a sign, a memory, for those who after us passing by might share the same joy, our happiness towards life.

'Without me for thousands of years the rose will blossom and the spring will bloom, but those who have secretly understood my heart will approach and visit the grave where I lie'.

But walking can also take you from mountain to mountain, without a final destination, in the continuous search for something new, craving for knowledge down the streets of the world.

Who will have learned more about life, those who have walked up and down the mountains or sailed across the seas without a point of arrival, or those who once arrived at the end of the enchanted vale have set their dwelling and put down roots?

I take Amlêt by the arm with a smooth contact, just to caress him lightly. Amlêt follows me dragging his body ahead, without vigor, without strength. Outside the building we set out behind Horatio along alleys he only knows. The day is getting a little misty, it has lost the summer brightness of the morning. When we walk past the church of Saint Mary, the bell-tower clock strikes two in the afternoon. A sharp thud which leaves me as suspended for a while, a moment of reflection, of distress. Our minutes hasten to their end.

CAMINO TWO IN THE AFTERNOON

The bell-tower clock of All Saints church in Camino al Tagliamento strikes two in the afternoon when Carmela wakes up. Lying in bed, she watches the light filtering through the chinks of the shutter. Outside it's broad daylight. Her first thought is for the director, for her new love: sound body, … Jesus … closing my eyes and taking a deep breath … enjoying life. He makes me feel more of a woman, more considered. Guglielmo isn't like this. Al least the poor husband of mine might have called … what did it cost him? Nothing. That's his nature. He prefers to stay alone, to avoid troubles. He prefers to give up living to avoid inconvenience. But I am not forty yet, and don't give up, don't stop. I've never stopped in my life. It is as though I have lived lots of different lives. When I sensed that something didn't work, I immediately got rid of that weight. A lot of lives, but actually just one, and I can't see why I shouldn't enjoy it now I am in the summer of my years. Seize the day. If it doesn't work any more with Guglielmo, we'll have to look for what is nice and positive in this moment, without imagining that tomorrow things will be better and everything will come out right… Rubbish! It isn't that way. I like feeling the man near me, who gives importance to me. I like feeling a strong back that gives me support, relief. You must give the man the appearance that he's got the initiative, he decides things for you, in order to have him at your feet. With Guglielmo a cold bed. Maybe, we'll see, I don't know, and never yes, yes, yes. Thousands of hesitations, and it isn't that way you make a woman happy. Not like the other, my director. Tonight I'll stay at his home. I've never done it since I met

Guglielmo, but you change course. Go where the wind takes you. He is in London in search of his fortune, and I am lying in bed with my boss. When we make love, I realize he is completely mine, willing to do anything for me. In that total abandonment I'm feeling like dying, and I'd like those moments to last forever, endlessly. A drug which helps me, makes me feel good. Moments which crown me the queen of the universe, unique. They are all my life. I get mother of a new world. I am a poor woman, I admit it, but those moments give me essence, courage, they help me carry on, accept the downfalls life has in store, because I feel inside the strength of a mantis which creates and destroys, gives life and death, mistress of its own destiny. After the death of our poor baby, Guglielmo stopped living. Instead, I never stop, and my rage makes me run even faster. I've always thought you must say shit, shit, shit, when things don't work, and not God here, God there. Stay with the man who makes you feel good, who is willing to give you everything … as long as it lasts, after that it is another day and we'll see.

LUNCH AT PHOENIX HOSTEL

The Phoenix Hostel is the typical brownstone building, on two floors, with large, white sash windows and rather worn out casements. At the entrance, there is a sense of precariousness, the less you spend, the less you enjoy, but also something alternative which comes from the informal staff towards hosts, from the walls plastered over with posters, photos, invitations, information about the events in town, and from the atmosphere with a lot of young people who greet each other, willingly stop to talk, or simply enjoy staying together.

As soon as we enter, we immediately understand Horatio is a familiar figure, a considered person, loved for his culture, for his kind, respectful attitude towards everybody. Amlêt too in that lively environment has recovered a bit of vigor, of confidence, and curiously looks at that familiar world which in his life, particularly in the last few months, has never lived. Horatio accompanies us into a large sitting room with armchairs and sofas which have known the two world wars, full of young people who draw aside to make a bit of room for us. Amlêt and I find to sit down on two small armchairs near the window, while Horatio is sitting on a sofa near a beautiful, black girl of ten, eleven years of age, who has moved over to leave him a bit of room, and looks at him with warmth, showing the love a person has towards a father. Then she gets closer to him, as though to look for the affection of a caress. I watch the whole scene with curiosity. I'm feeling a bit embarrassed to find myself together with the young company of all ethnic groups and cultures, and I, around fifty, nearly the eldest. Horatio, in his sixties, is of comfort to me, makes me feel less alone, even though he seems to move in that world of young people with the self-assurance of a teenager. The living room where we are sitting communicates, through a passage with an arch, with the kitchen, from where we can hear a clinking of dishes and a coming and going of young people who are taking something from the fridge. We can't see the rings, but we can imagine somebody is cooking by the smell of food till the sitting room.

'Shall we have lunch here? I have got some chicken tacos in the fridge,' Horatio says to us.

He is the landlord there, and offers what is available in the communal fridge of the hostel. I know I am still in debt of breakfast, and by nature I am not used to taking advantage. I suggest going to buy something from a small supermarket we walked past to get to the hostel.

'You are my hosts. It's ready-made food, simply to heat in the microwave. Nothing to worry about!' Horatio says to me.

'I'd like to help, to contribute somehow...' I explain my concern to him.

'You can go and get some beer from the bar if you and your friend are not teetotalers … I'd like some beer and you?'

'Okay, that's fine.'

I don't usually drink beer, but it seems to me a nice solution, and I stand up to go and order the beer at the bar which is located near the entrance of the hostel. Standing to wait for my turn, I see a young man gazing at me with interest. Around thirty years of age, a nice appearance, short, tidy hair, designed shorts and clarks without socks, something different from the other hosts.

'You're Italians, aren't you?' the young man asks me.

'Yes, we are. How did you know it?'
'Well, with the Italians you can't be mistaken. We might be a bit superficial, but we are surely creative. The 'bella figura' is part of our dna. If we can afford it, we spend and we are more careful about our appearance than others.'
'I agree … where are you from?'
'From Spoleto.'
'Visiting London?'
'Not exactly. I've got a degree in architecture, but in Italy to find a job for what you studied is more and more a mirage.'
'Brain drain. Looking for a job in England?'
'Yes and no. I am taking a master on the Arts and Crafts movement by William Morris. You might not know it, but it is a topic which has always fascinated me...'
'Two bitters and a lager. Ten quid fifty,' the barman shouts and puts three mugs of beer on the bar. I take a note of ten pounds out of my wallet. One of the last. I can't but think my week in London is at risk if I can't control the spending.
'Listen! We haven't introduced ourselves. My name's Giuliano.'
'Guglielmo.'
'Guglielmo, why don't we make a good pasta? We teach these guys here how to cook it. Yesterday I saw some Germans put the pasta to cook in cold water!' he says to me with a sardonic laugh.
'All right, there are three of us over there, if it isn't too much trouble.'
'Puréed tomatoes, two olives and pasta what it needs. For one person or four, you just dirty one pot.'
'Okay, but I want to chip in. I'll inform my friends and order a beer for you as well. Right?'

'Sure.'

I take the beers down from the bar and go into the sitting room where I can't see Horatio any more. I put them down on the small table in front of Amlêt, who hasn't moved from the armchair. Lost in his world, he's murmuring something to himself, attracting the attention of the little girl in front who's staring at him a little worried.

'Amlêt, where's Horatio?' I ask him.

With a wave he hints at the kitchen where I can see him occupied with heating the chicken tacos in the microwave. I go into the kitchen where there is a crowd of other busy youths: some of them are standing and eating a bite, others are washing some dishes in the sink, others are keeping an eye on something boiling in the pot and Horatio is busy with his tacos.

'Horatio, I met an Italian young man in the bar. You might know him as well. He offered to cook spaghetti for all of us. Together.' I inform him about the meeting with Giuliano.

'Okay. That's fine. Spaghetti and tacos then. We'll have a complete meal.'

In that moment the Italian comes into the kitchen with the spaghetti and everything necessary to make tomato pasta. He's been at the hostel for a few weeks, and has already exchanged some words with Horatio who immediately greets him. He starts working right away, and shows he knows the place well, and he also has got a certain ability in the kitchen. I stand near him ready to give a hand if necessary.

COMPARISON BETWEEN GENERATIONS

It is common in similar situations, when you meet a young Italian abroad, to start talking about Italy, about the main political and social events, about the changes occurred in the last few months.
'I won't go back to Italy any more. Sure! I'd rather start doing the washing up, any work here in London,' Giuliano explains to me.
'It would be useful for young people to remain in Italy, wouldn't it? To change things …'
'In Italy things will never change. Young people are discouraged and most of them don't think it is possible to find a job, lead a normal life, marry and set up house …'
'Considering my present situation I can't say you are wrong, even though I belong to a different generation. But when I was your age, it wasn't like this.'
'I know, the political crisis in the seventies and nineties, the protest in the universities and the fight in the factories … My father well instructed me on these things.'
'Indeed, I forgot you might be my son, and your father one of my peers. But for me too everything is different now. Believe me!'
Till the age of this young man here, the sense of belonging to a left political party was related to everything that was young, intense, intelligent, resourceful. However, already at that time, during my solitary ramblings in the mountains, I stopped to look at the peaks white with snow which rose up into the deep blue sky, and I thought the mountains had been there for millions of years, and up the same rocks, before me, the primitive men had climbed, and before them forms of life gone forever. And in the

evening I used to go walking in the countryside to contemplate the starry sky, and I thought about the infinite space of the universe, where the nearest star, the Proxima Centauri, is four light-years away, billions and billions of kilometers, and what we see now with our telescopes is a world which existed millions of years behind. Thinking about all this, a man gets scared, and meditates on how relative our efforts to change the world are, considering our short existence, our fragile nature, how limited we are in time and space. When you look at the tiny ant which runs all alone up the mountain, or behind thousands of other tiny ants, you unconsciously crush who knows how many, you wonder how they ended up there and which their goal is. At least, those I have in my vegetable garden cultivate lice on cucumber shoots, they have something to do, even though they do damage, and with a poison squirt I kill thousands. *Gas! Gas! An ecstasy of fumbling.* Are we like this as well? The evolution of the chaos which is the universe. And so, politics, economics, my commitment to do things thinking the achievements were forever, they were eternal, little by little dwindled, they turned out to be an illusion, like our science, our inventions and so on. The universe is indifferent to our toil, to our economic and social improvements, to our exertion to change the world.

'When I was your age, left ideology was a shared belief by most of young people. There were great expectations and the idea to change the world inside a party seemed a possible reality. And then …' I can't finish my analysis that Giuliano interrupts me.

'And then in a more and more global reality, you found yourselves older and in a world which was going to the opposite of the expected direction. The same litany I've heard I don't know how often from my parents.'

'Oh yes. A bad awakening.'
I started thinking of the mistake of those political meetings to talk about people we didn't know. Comrades from the other part of the world we would have liked to free from slavery, worried of their misery, of their unhappiness. And to search for other people's happiness, we were not good at enjoying our own happiness any more. The incapability of enjoying the simple things life has in store for us.
Politics, social commitment made us consider only the future of a global world, instead of living the present reality which is near us. I started thinking that my link to party ideology, the total political commitment gave me a sense of annoyance. The conviction I was losing my time in meaningless things made me consider the idea of having my own family with a child who runs about you, who has everything to learn. I was very confused. My priority became to look for a job, the love of a wife, the company of a son. But the son hasn't come and love to my wife has recently dwindled. And I realize the idea of being part of a community, of living experiences together, of sharing projects doesn't exist in my life any more. I'm feeling alone, without ideas, without the desire of starting anew.
Even now, when I look at the mountains which brighten in the morning sun, I think they've been there for millions of years, and we, with our short lives of passion and sorrow, are nothing. I remain quiet to gaze at the mountains which kindle in the setting sun.
Nothing to be done.
'May I ask you, if you don't bother, what you are doing here in London,' Giuliano suddenly asks me.
How can I explain my situation, the reason of my presence here in London, to a young man who urges to change

things, who still trusts people's intelligence? He will never understand it. Above all, a clever youth who looks with suspicion, with critical sense, at his parents' generation who created a blocked system, where to step down in favor of the young is almost impossible. They are denied hope, a real, social recognition. To a competent person like this young man here, the parochialism, the superficiality, the ignorance which brought a nobody like me to London, might look like piss-taking, the irony of a sick world.

'I am in London to interview a retired, university professor, a Shakespeare critic who taught in Italy for many years,' I reply with a certain hesitation.

'Are you paid by the university or is it your personal initiative?' he asks me.

'They give me something … There's also my personal interest,' I say to him trying to hide my lying.

'I too was trying to do something at the university of Perugia, but the system was so blocked, and the possibility of getting on reduced to nothing … I gave up.'

Giuliano turns round to check the pasta, and the conversation ends up there, without the shame of explaining to him I am still a teacher on a short-term contract, and I go round from school to school, where they send me. A situation I live with frustration and try to hide, even though it always leaves inside of me a malaise difficult to endure.

'I've finished here. The pasta is ready. Have a look about the dishes and the cutlery, whether Horatio has thought of it?'

'I saw Horatio doing it.'

'Okay. Then help me strain the pasta. The English don't know the strainer and we'll have to cope somehow,' Giuliano says to me with a sarcastic laugh.

Around the table, in the farthest corner of the sitting room, Horatio is entertaining the company. Sitting between Amlêt and the young girl, he's telling them something amusing. Everybody is laughing happily. A moment of consolation after the disappointment of the morning. On the table nothing is really missing: the dishes with the pasta, the chicken tacos, the beers, and the eyes of the little girl which are beaming happily. Even Amlêt is showing more vivacity, and the joyful company is beneficial to him. Horatio is the master of the house, and wanted to recreate the familiar atmosphere of sharing which is generally found in hostels.

He's come to sit near me. He knows he must give an explanation about the little black girl who is sitting with us. Giuliano didn't care about that extra dish on the table, and everybody seems to enjoy the merriment the good food has brought, with no worries.

All the same, Horatio values to explain to his Italian friends the new image of himself he found in the hostel. Here, he wanted to make his knowledge of human nature, the experience of a wise man, who has been all over the world, available to others. After long voyaging from one harbor to another, the hostel represents his home. He tells us about the meeting with the girl sitting near him. A salvific meeting which proves that by helping people in need, you also help yourself.

'When I first came to this hostel six, seven years ago, there was this deaf-mute girl, Abidal is her name, just abandoned by her mother. The poor woman was ordered to leave the country, being illegally in the UK and accused of drugs trafficking,' Horatio heartily says to us.

'The only possibility for the girl to stay in England was to separate her from her mother. She was five then and had started going to school. Well, I decided to take care of her. I am her foster grandpa, and she adores me now. She's become a nice girl. I hope that sooner or later her mum will turn up and reclaim her. I am here now, her grandpa!' says Horatio in an emotional tone.

The girl realizes Horatio has talked about her, and gets closer to him with all the love and affection she can show to the man who helps her grow up. Giuliano and I have followed Horatio's confession with attention and we share it with words of encouragement. His choice, the promise made to her mother to look after her as long as she comes back to London, touches everybody's heart.

I am in front of an example of the philosophy I've always craved for: to love the people near you, share with them your beautiful memories, your happiness, but also your deep sorrows and regrets, because the world will get on its own way and only those moments will be important in the end. With the progress of time also those feelings will dwindle and disappear with us, when we get old and die. Philosophies, moral systems, ideologies are like the peaks of mountains outside clouds, seen at a great distance, none higher, more important, more truthful than others, but life is down here, with those who love you and are close to you.

After the joyful lunch all together, it is time of farewells which for Horatio and Giuliano means going back to every day's normal life, for me, instead, there is the disappointment of one more failure, that is, the matter of my visit to London searching for professor Brough and the evidence of Friulian Hamlet. Everything has turned out to be fake news as I suspected. After saying goodbye to Giuliano and exchanging with him reciprocal wishes of professional success and of prosperity to poor, unfortunate

Italy, I am standing in front of Horatio, my English friend, undecided about what to do. Just a moment, because Horatio takes my hand and holds it with affection. We understand it hasn't been an occasional meeting, we would have many other things to say to each other, but life makes us continue our path, with the load of responsibilities we all carry behind. To Horatio, the few hours spent together were enough to understand my character, my difficulty, the failure of my endeavor in London.

'If you need my help tomorrow, I am here. We might try seeing mister Brough again,' says Horatio.

'I don't know. I'm rather skeptical,' I say to him.

'Senile dementia has got many returns.'

'Yes, but still I am quite doubtful the professor might come to his senses again.'

'I see, but we are friends now, and you know where I am staying and … just in case …'

'Thank you, Horatio. You are a real friend.'

'Oh. You are welcome.'

Horatio goes to say goodbye to Amlêt, who has always been sitting at the table, entered his parallel world. He's pulled up his knees on the chair, and mutters something to himself, his sight on a sunbeam entering through the open window. Sitting in front of him, the little, deaf-mute girl is looking at the young man with interest, and it seems she might have understood the enter key of Amlêt's world, the thread of his thoughts, in the quiet of her silent world.

Horatio doesn't know anything of Amlêt's problems, and hasn't fully understood what is the bond between us. He looks for the young man's hand to greet him, but Amlêt doesn't understand, doesn't hear, doesn't mind. Then Horatio gives him just a pat on his shoulder which makes him jump up to his feet and pull away from him, as if he's seen the devil in person.

I take Amlêt by the arm and waving goodbye to friends, I accompany him out of the hostel with all the tact needed.

When we are alone in the street, I start thinking about Horatio's discourse, his helpfulness, his sign of friendship to me, and I realize something is changing inside me. I am strongly feeling my responsibility to Amlêt, the prospect of another life, different, Horatio well showed to me with his example.

AFTERNOON IN LONDON

The bell-tower clock of the Christ Church of England in Bell street strikes five in the afternoon. The weather outside has changed, and a nasty wind seems to bring near a storm. I don't know what to do exactly. I realize I can't engage Horatio in my personal matters. I also know I've got a great responsibility towards Amlêt. This moral commitment is getting more and more important. It isn't just Amlêt who needs me, but it's getting a reciprocal matter. I'm feeling inside the benefits of his presence.

Now I need to invent something to get out of the complicated situation we are in. Instinctively, I remember I am in a borough I knew very well when I worked in London, and I feel like going back of twenty years, to the swinging London of my youth. Why not show Amlêt something about the places which are so familiar to me, which I know so well, and share with him memories, emotions of those distant years, my post-degree time, when I was in England to improve my English? I was more or less as old as Amlêt is now, and worked in a pub to the north of Regent's Park, not far from Hampstead, the most beautiful part of London. I still see myself behind the bar of 'The George', that was the name of the pub, in Haverstock Hill, to serve mugs of lager and bitter and lime. I still remember the way many times I walked to go to the center, as far as Marble Arch, down Belsize Grove, Primrose Hill, Regent's Park. Wonderful time! The pub is a bit far and it takes almost an hour on foot. I don't know whether Amlêt is used to walking so long. The temperature is ideal with the breeze which has cooled the late afternoon.

'Amlêt, do you want to go for a walk with me, around the London I know well?' I ask him.

Amlêt doesn't reply, but he follows me and it seems he has no alternative.

'They are the places where I worked when I was your age,' I say to him while walking towards Park Road.

'Memories are what keeps us alive, when we are stuck and can't find the way to go on …'

It is a monologue, but Amlêt is listening to me and walking behind at a good pace. The people we meet are coming back from work, queuing in front of the bus stop or hurrying down the stairs to catch the underground train. An hour or maybe longer to get home, to Greater London.

A crowd pushes forward to a kiosk on the pavement, to stuff themselves with a burger, a bite of two pounds, guzzled while standing. Other people are queuing in front of a cinema for the tickets of the show on the bill. Another group is waiting to consume the last illusion, the great hit, the concert of their idol in a venue nearby.

The fresh air of dusk has cleared away the stormy clouds, but it has blown waste everywhere. Plastic bags, newspaper sheets are flying away before falling down on a mound of rubbish, under the glare of commercial lighting.

A lonely young woman, sitting on a bench inside Regent's Park, is busy doing something on her smartphone. Sad, watery eyes, tired of drunkenness and excess. She glances at passers-by, but can't see anybody. She stands up and sets off for home, lolling her head, a bored expression, stranger to everything around her.

THE GEORGE PUB

It is almost seven in the evening when down Primrose Hill Road we are getting near the pub where I worked for three months. 'The George', I remember it well, was a bit different from the other London pubs. It had more light in the inner rooms and the windows let you see outside. Above the entrance door the sign *The George*, with nearby the drawing of a crown. Maybe in honor of the stuttering king, George VI, the one of the film starring Colin Firth. A king adored by his citizens during the Second World War. There are always a lot of people standing outside, in summer and winter, for a chat about soccer or a puff, with the mugs of beer put on barrels placed at the entrance. From half past four till seven in the evening, with the Happy Hour, there is no room both inside and outside, above all in fine weather. When we enter, I immediately remember the typical smell of beer spilled on the carpet. I go among the standing customers to the bar. Amlêt follows me. I am curious to see whether there is still my old boss, but I don't recognize a soul there any more. I'm told he sold the pub ten years before, and they know nothing about him any more.

I intend to eat something and get some peace for a while, but inside there's no room, not even standing. Undecided about what to do, I glance at Amlêt, squeezed among customers speaking out in the din of the place. I am on the point of going out, when two women, sitting alone in a corner of the pub, beckon us to get comfortable at their table. We have no choice. Not even at the bar you find room to order. We sit down near the two English young women. Amlêt, to the right of a fleshy youth, around thirty years of age, with a round, nice face, short, curly hair, neatly dressed, the tight skirt above her knees and a fantasy t-shirt with two pippins well in sight ahead. She sips a gin tonic near the end. The young woman sitting to my right is a robust, broad-shouldered type. She has strong hips well marked by her tight jeans, quite a dull expression, a plain face surrounded by long hair down her shoulders. In front of her a pint of beer almost full. You might guess it isn't the first. They laugh happily, but it is always the chubby one to murmur something, while the other, maybe already stoned, keeps giggling like a fool. You can guess that we two are the center of their conversation.

When the waiter comes to us, I order two pints of lager without thinking. Maybe in my sub-conscious I don't want to be less than the two ladies here, or maybe in my recollections as a waiter in that pub, to drink just half a pint you are really ill. I also think that Amlêt didn't even touch his beer at Phoenix Hostel. Quite strange, if I think that in Friuli, before leaving, he was used to drinking like a sponge. I also notice that the youth, hardly used to staying near a woman, is sitting quite stiff, a fixed gaze into the void in front. And by sheer coincidence, the young woman on heat has got closer to provoke him a bit.

'Italians? Oh! I love Italy!' the curly woman speaks out after we introduced one another on their request.

'He's a nice bloke … the young man,' she mumbles to her mate, with the intention of making herself understood by me as well. Her mate limits herself to a silly giggle, concentrated on her beer. She seems tipsy, able to understand only part of what is going on. Amlêt has started to stare at a big man nearby, a big stomach. He vehemently tinkers with a slot machine, a slap on the colored screen to vent his fury. He can't start again. He feels like a woman to ease his frustration. He glances at a lass he knows well. She's sitting at the bar. He goes to her, his hand on her fleshy thigh out of the miniskirt. He has to show all his vanity. She looks at him absent-mindedly, and he makes a welcome of indifference.

The waiter comes with the beers. We'll have to wait for the burgers. I swallow a few drafts, but Amlêt doesn't move from his chair. He's sitting straight as a poker, hands on his knees, intimidated by the advances of the curly young woman who moves forward with her chair, her body almost in contact with the youth. Her hands move freely on the hem of her miniskirt, on her knees, to smooth her curly hair, in an attitude of strong seduction. As soon as our eyes meet, she recovers a certain propriety and distances her chair again. Also the big young woman near me, though with slow and heavy movements, furtively casts a glance at me waiting for a reaction.

'It's flat! … His cock I mean … seen it?' says the curly woman to her mate who just giggles stupidly. Her intention is to be heard by me in order to study my reaction. They realize that there is something wrong with Amlêt.

'He is without feeling … a piece of wood …' Words said in a low voice to her mate, but loud enough to be heard by me as well.

I feel responsible about Amlêt's situation, and I don't know what sort of reaction he might have in that moment of deep, mental distress.

It's almost nine in the evening when at last they serve the burgers. I start eating it after taking a long draft of beer. Amlêt doesn't touch the burger, he remains stuck, nailed to his chair, really disturbed.

I don't feel like encouraging such a cheeky, absurd situation, taking advantage of the women's complaisance. I care about Amlêt's moment and not even for fun I want to comply with the two English women's desire, so mechanical, without passion.

After finishing the burger and taking a draft of beer, I stand up with politeness in order not to give rise to sardonic comments, and hint at Amlêt to follow me to the exit. The youth comes behind me saying nothing, and leaves the burger and the beer on the table.

'The Italians are sneaking out … Fucking Latin lovers!'

Expression accompanied by a mocking laugh by the two women who didn't imagine such an unexpected conclusion.

TOWARDS HAMPSTEAD GREEN

It's almost dark when we get outside. Again, I'll have to invent something to give meaning to such a hard day.

Fleeting clouds from the Atlantic are passing before the face of the crescent moon just risen over the buildings. The evening is nice. You feel good outside. We are not far from Hampstead Heath, where I used to spend an hour before starting the afternoon shift at the pub. A quarter of an hour on foot to get to Parliament Hill Viewpoint, where the view of London is magnificent. Over there, sitting on a bench, I used to spend time reading or writing about my homesickness, the separation from friends.

We are taking the shortest way to Hampstead Green, when the belfry clock of Saint Stephen's Rosslyn Hill church strikes ten. Amlêt is now quite relieved, and follows me amused of our roaming around London by night. In that quiet area of London you walk well. There aren't many people about, just a few ladies of the night in front of the clubs, and rare people who come back home from work, from walking the dog, from entertainments in a London not so popular with tourists.

We enter the park and go uphill for a while, towards Parliament Hill Viewpoint. I still remember the benches with an immense view of the city lights in the dark of night. I've got an enchanting memory when after work, after eleven in the evening, I ended up there with the sweetheart I had in London. Another world, other people, a suitcase full of dreams, sitting on a bench, hugging my beloved, in the center of Hampstead Park at nightfall. London lights down south and a swarm of stars twinkling in the sky over the great city. It is as being a kid again, unable to count all the stars on the fingers of my hand, or seeing myself as a lad, lying on the dewy grass and gazing at the August sky, the shooting stars. A sparkle in the firmament, with a handful of desires which fade far away. A never-grown child, a head full of dreams, afraid of facing life without the certainty of a father near you who accompanies you to the discovery of the world. Together watching mid-August shooting stars, so distant in the sky, at the end of summer.

Strange that it's really me who would have liked to be a father, would have liked to have a son, I am now being the father of this poor youth, Amlêt, lost in his world, lost in a foreign London. We two are sitting here on the same bench after twenty years, gazing at mid-August shooting stars.

'Amlêt, when I was your age I often used to come exactly to the same place where we are sitting now, at Parliament Hill Viewpoint …'

'I've never been here in my wild wandering around London of the last few months. It has never happened to me to come up here.'

'Sure. The agencies generally promote only the West End and the City of London, and it is there where all tourists gather, it is there where legal and illegal business is done.'

'It is not fair,' he says to me. Maybe bewitched by the place, by the quiet of the night, by the twinkling of lights far away, Amlêt is now listening to me, he is present and not a pilgrim in his strange and distant world.

'If you want to know the real London,' I say to him, 'you must come here to the north, up narrow streets till Hampstead Heath, as we did tonight.'

'Far from anybody? … Alone? I don't know whether I like it … After all, I enjoy losing myself among people.

Anonymous people who don't look at you with suspicion, don't judge you and don't make you think you are different.'

'Sure. People are of all kinds. Still in Greater London, places like Hampstead don't lose touch with our true nature, invite you to rest, make you consider your present situation, who you are and where you are going. And it is even easier to find someone who can give you a hand.'

'Or he thinks you are mad … I don't know what makes them believe to be superior, to judge ...'

'Don't believe it, Amlêt, we are often prejudiced because we don't know ourselves well enough, and we don't have time to know the others, to feel the contact of those who are near us … For superficiality … We'll have to start from here.'

'I am not that sure.'

'Believe me! It's luck if you meet someone who spends time listening to you, ready to give you a hand in need.'

A long stillness, just the distant noise of the city which is abating.

'Tonight, I really like to be here with you and not alone, after the disappointment of professor Brough.'

'That matter seems so funny to me. What does Shakespeare have to do with Camino al Tagliamento and the Committee?'

'If you too think so …' I contain myself in order not to talk nonsense. After a short pause I continue. 'According to the theory of the Committee for Friulian Hamlet, Shakespeare knew the story of the marquis da Camino well, and to give substance to their conviction, they invented professor Brough's study.'

'I bet that they dragged me too into their scheme,' Amlêt says to me.

'Sure! You and the poor, old professor who, as we have seen, can't confirm anything.'
'They've had what they deserve!'
'Still, as far as I am concerned, this case has changed me inside. The air of Greater London after so long, the meeting with Horatio, his beautiful story with that girl, professor Brough's present wretchedness, after his luminous past as a scholar, and the meeting with you, Amlêt, here in London, one case out of a million, mean something …'
After a moment of deep internal anguish.
'I don't know whether I want to return to Camino, I don't know whether I want to return to my wife. I've been feeling so lonely in the last few months, and I thank you again for your company. It makes me feel less desperate. We two, Amlêt, will have to start something together again. A strange case, I'd say an almost impossible coincidence, put us together in this moment of difficulty of both of us. It must mean something. We'll have to look together for positive examples to start again. I think it is still possible … for both of us. Horatio had been round the whole world, taught in all latitudes and came back home, and here in London he has found his fulfillment. His experiences helped him to look for the right way, and he's a happy person who at sixty still finds enthusiasm, emotions, will to live. As long as we can, we mustn't become a number like professor Brough. As long as we can.'
Amlêt hasn't understood well my long discourse, but still he's got the perception of being important. Maybe for the first time in his life he is feeling treated as equal. He's looking over there at the lights of Greater London in the dark, far away, anonymous, cold, and here, sitting next to

him a man who is asking for help. An innocent, teasing
tear is running down his face.

'Amlêt, I've almost forgotten that today is the tenth of August, Saint Lawrence night, and from up here we might look at the shooting stars … if the sky hadn't got cloudy again.'
'I too did it when I was a boy, but I never saw anything.'
'You didn't look at the right side … that corner of sky towards north-east. I remember I was sitting on the same bench twenty years ago. I'd like to consider past time again, and see whether it is still possible to have desires. We are two unlucky cases. We haven't had much from life. Thinking about all my journey, about the fact that I led you up here to show you this place where I felt good, in order to live emotions I had in the past, might be an experience which helps me, which helps us a lot. A person who listens to you might be of great comfort … might help you as well. Amlêt, you are young, I've already told you, but still you've got the experience of an unhappy life, spent in solitude wandering about the underworld, about the city slums, where the most diverse mob lives.'
'I've been roaming about London for months on my quest for revenge, for retaliation on the people who don't' consider me, who have never considered me as I am, and instead of giving a hand, they shout you out even more and you are passed for a misfit …'
'Amlêt, your malcontent shows a strong desire to change things. All of us have got dreams, hidden aspirations we ask the Magi Star …'
'Not me!'
'It must be something you wish for, a concealed desire …'
'To calm the fears inside me, the anger which suffocates

me … yes that.'

'See, you remember things. You know your hidden desires...'

'Getting over the continuous obsession of my father, dangling beneath the beams of the barn, who keeps telling me you are a failure, a good-for-nothing. I mustn't listen to people, old friends who stare at me with mockery, laugh at me, place a glass of wine in front and say, Amlêt, tell us about your relations with the Lords from Treviso. Why is it that everybody calls you Count, though in truth you have got nobody to count on?'

'They mock you!'

'They've always done it since I was a boy. Yes, I've got wishes … Even in my worst moments, when the world gets all dark and I want to kill myself, to end up with this wicked world, or when I see myself as the violated dauphin, the only marquis prince of the da Camino, ready to revenge my father killed by his murderer brother, even in those moments, I can see a tremulous light in the distance, the strong desire to be like everybody, to have a right to a normal life, to succeed in getting out of this prison, to find a corner in the sun, mine, only mine, and find a person who gives me a hand, who accepts me the way I am, and together start a new course of life. Yes, this is my wish. This is what I ask the Magi star. It won't be easy because I don't like myself any more.'

'I like your wishes, which are for a fairer world, where there is respect for everybody. No ambition, only a fairer world towards the people in difficulty.'

Amlêt looks at me with the satisfaction of being understood, of finding a person who is listening to him. A luck which has never occurred before in his life. A thrill of happiness seizes all his body. He remains waiting, as if to make this moment last longer, with the hope it will never end. It is the confession of a wise man, and I, from psychoanalyst I become a patient.

'Amlêt, a wish of mine, I've kept inside of me, has always been to have a son. Maybe because I lost my infant son. Doctors always look for thousands of causes to explain facts. It is difficult to keep up with them. I'm thinking now how my life's changed since my son's death. It hasn't been a change in the body, rather how you see the world. Even now, after so many years, it infuriates me to think how our human nature leads us to forget. It isn't superficiality as common people might think. For years lots of them were near us, my wife and I, they did everything to make us forget. Every festive occasion they invited us, in order not to let us alone. Gifts, Christmas lights, snow longing at the window, always somebody around, when you want to be alone to feed on nothing, without being obliged to do things. People, relatives were worried to see us alone. Our life started again to run after silly things, day by day: soccer, television, politics, the news … And when I thought of my son in my arms, suddenly I felt a void inside, I felt dizzy and the sensation to sink into an abyss. Without a reason, without knowing why, just a mechanism had gone wrong, a stupid spring gone off. It was pointless to wonder why. Belief in life, in God who sees and attends to everything, a way to start living again, to return to your old habits, put on the usual mask when you go out among people, and back home to return yourself again in the solitude of your room. And you see those moments again and again as if they were now. The same scene with the same eyes as that time. Yes, that fact changed my life. I've always considered it an absurdity, a fatal injustice. It has always vexed me deeply. And even now after so many years it has left a void inside … and the wish to have a son, and…'

'Stop it! Stop it!' Amlêt shouts in the dark of the night. 'Leave me alone! I don't want to hear any more!' Amlêt isn't here any more. He doesn't know what a father means so well. He's never had one. He grew up with his grandpa, and used to see his father back from the pub only in the evening. He emitted a grunt, never a word of comfort, a word of encouragement, a caress. Never.

'Amlêt, mine is just a wish, a mid-August shooting star which falls away, a mid-summer night's dream, a light beam to give force and vigor to a hidden desire, never fulfilled. Like tonight, on the tenth of August, in lots of hamlets in Carnia they throw burning discs of wood high, and send them rolling down the hill. They've always done it for centuries in mid-summer. I remember when we would go outside the parish church of Gorto, on the vigil of the Assumption, to wait for the event in the rain. 'Go, go, go this nice disk …' And it rushed down the hill along the wire to the final thud at the end of the run. In the old days it wasn't like today, a folkloric manifestation, but it marked a moment of passage, the beginning of a new cycle, either a relationship between a lad and a lass, 'In honor and in favor …' or a friendship, a new period as it might be for us, Amlêt, who can't take this wicked world here any more. I've always wondered whether it was possible to cancel my life up to now, and begin a new one … impossible … Anyway, I'd begin from Carnia, that abandoned land, where you can live in peace with yourself. The nice, burning disc which rolls down fast to imitate the sun which governs all the process of life would take me there. What is better than a piece of land, you are given for little money, and start doing what you like, without masters which control you …'

'People who are in command, who look at what you're doing, who judge you … are everywhere.' I am surprised to see Amlêt has followed my discourse.

'Those people will always be, but only us would be the masters of our fate. And we can see in spring that everything comes to life again: the cherry trees you planted in bloom, the little plant which from the ground springs up to light, and the sun watches all the produce of the land grow and ripen in the summer heat. And you see behind you something important made with your own hands, with your work, your talent. The feeling of a dignified life, free, in an environment to the measure of man, with your ancestors looking at you from above, happy to see Carnia thrive as in the old days. In a traditional vision where you return to the artisan, to small organizations of workers, where the belief is humanitarian, based on the value that people are more important than material things. The people who are near you, who love you … What do you think, Amlêt? Is that possible?'

'As at the time of my ancestors, the marquis from Treviso, in the Middle Ages,' replies Amlêt, with a consideration that sounds more sensible than mine.

'Yes, you are right, but with the freedom to decide, to move freely, to choose who to stay with, and not like the peasant serfs of your masters, the da Camino, with no rights, tied to their lords for generations and generations, without the possibility of redemption.'

'They were not good people, my ancestors from Treviso. I myself have read this. When I see them in front, they ask me to forgive them of their mischiefs, of their murders. And my father too, when I dream of him dangling beneath the beams of the barn, he asks me to forgive him, to love him despite all he did to me. After all, he wasn't a bad man … Abandoned by my mother with me still a little child. He didn't have an easy life, either. But I don't want to go back to Camino. Nobody likes me in Camino. Amlêt, the lunatic who wanders alone down the river banks, and says he is a prince.'

'Neither do I, Amlêt. I don't want to go back to Camino. Mission impossible. I'll write to the president of the Committee for Friulian Hamlet about the present condition of professor Brough. To Carmela … I don't know … she might have understood … I need time to think. I'm sure she's arranged something elsewhere. I'm certain about this. She isn't short of company.'

A little light starts to give shape to the world around, on Westminster, on the dome of Saint Paul's, on the distant buildings towards the Thames which disappears down the plane to the sea. Amlêt and I get going towards our new tomorrow, where the Magi star will lead us. It turns and turns and leads us to places where the sun warms and people are near you, respect you, love you. Dreaming of a different world, imagining a different life, because we are such stuff as dreams are made on, and our little life is rounded with a sleep. We two, together, Amlêt, Guglielmo, and all those who are near us and love us. In the belief we'll be living the show of life till the curtain drops and everything fades away and leaves not a rack behind.

And this weak and idle theme,
No more yielding but a dream,
Gentles, do not reprehend.
If you pardon, we will mend.

(A Midsummer Night's Dream)

Table of Contents

Graziano Urli

IL CÂS DAL AMLÊT FURLAN

Storie sucedude a Londre, un 10 di Avost dal gnûf mileni

TAL OSTEL SAINT JAMES

Distirât sul jet dal ostel Saint James di Earls Court, o cîr di durmî une lusigne, ma a son tancj i fats da la zornade, lis tensions che mi balin tal cjâf. Partît di buinore di Codroip sul tren par Trevîs, e dopo cul aeroplan Ryanair, cjamât come saradelis in scjatule, fin a Londre. A Trevîs, mi met in code pal check in, pe sigurece, dulà che ti palpin pardut. Gjave lis scarpis, met il portatil tal zei, e il Smart dulà diaul isal lât a finîle? Ta la gjachete, ce mone! Ce vuelino cumò? Forsi ur ai ridût daûr e a vuelin fâ viodi che a son lôr a comandâ.
'Si ritolga le scarpe e favorisca i documenti.' Ancje i talians si metin a rompi i tabars cumò!
Sul aeroplan i stewards si movevin sù e jù di un continui: l'aperitîf, il snack, il duty free, la loterie, i biliets pai teatris, pai museus di Londre e ce saio jò? Nol è un biel mistîr. Forsi a cjaparan un franc di plui, une percentuâl su ce che a vendin, ma a son passâts i timps cuant che chei di Alitalia a stavin trê dîs a New York, prime di tornâ indaûr. La stanchezza dei voli intercontinentali, il jet lag, lavoro a rischio, in pension a cuarante agns ... Mighe stupits! Cumò no se passin trop ben nancje lôr.
Fin al aeropuart di Stansted avonde ben, ma dopo in tren pe stazion Victoria, mi àn tirât il prin tacon. Cuasi un colp mortâl a la piçule risierve di bêçs che mi soi puartât daûr di cjase cu la idee di tirâ indelunc une setemane a Londre.
Cuindis sterlinis! Laris! Masse tart par lâ a cirî alc di alternatîf, e strac cence fâ nuie.
Se o jerin cuatri, cinc di nô, o podevin cjapâ il taxi neri, l'Austin Morris, come in gjite cu la scuele. Ducj ingrumâts daûr par sparagnâ un franc.

'Maledets talians!' al mugugnà il tassist, pensant che no lu varessin capît.

Il siôr che al duar sul jet a cjistiel sot di me al è rivât tal dormitori che nol è tant, si è butât jù vistût e indurmidît di strade.

Une puce di vinace di fâ ingomit. Al à tacât a ronfâ di fâ movi il linçûl che al pendole parsot dal gno jet.

Il siôr che al duar parsore al jere za li cuant ch'o soi jentrât te cjamare, e no si è mot di in chê volte. Un grum di peçots. O ai provât a alçâmi in ponte di pîts par viodi se al durmive, se al faseve fente, o se al jere un cadavar come tai films. I soi lât dongje par viodi se al respirave inmò. Il moviment a pene percepibil da lis spalis che si alçavin e sbassavin cul respîr, mancumâl, al jere ancjemò vîf.

A la reception dal ostel, mi àn tirât il secont tacon.

'Paiament anticipât,' mi à dit la impleade.

No mi vanzin tancj bêçs se o scuen paiâ dute la setemane in anticip. Jê no à sintude reson: o cussì o tu sgomis. Dopo, mi à dât une sacume di linçûl che a pene jentrât tal dormitori vincjecinc, cence un fregul di lûs, cun chel parsore che no savevi se al jere sveât, o muart incudulît, i ai metût un cuart d'ore par viodi cuâl che al jere il dret o il ledrôs. Tai ostei al fâs simpri un cjalt dal diaul, istât e invier, di tignî il barcon a ghiliotine un fregul viert, cul casin continui da la citât difûr, e tirâ la orele par sintî ce dal diaul che al è chel rumôr che nol ferme un moment, cu la sirene da la ambulance lontane. Un biel azart rivâ fin tal ospedâl plui dongje cul trafic. Miôr l'elicotar dal cent e disevot che i met un moment, ma dopo dulà si poie a Londre? Un biel probleme! La sirene da la polizie si è fermade propit denant dal ostel. A varan puartât dentri cualchi rufian si spere, cun chê sdrume di fantatis su lis stradis, tantis orientâls, di no capî ben di dulà che a son,

dutis compagnis, tailandesis, birmanis ... No si clame plui cussì il lôr paîs, Myanmar, une robe cussì. A jerin pardut. Si jere fin vicinade une nerute fûr da la stazion Victoria. 'Ti vuei ben!' mi à dit.
'Ancje jo fione, ma cun cuâi bêçs? Cence solts, Jude boie!' i ai mostradis lis sachetis tirant sù un tic lis spalis. Si è metude a ridi e mi à dit alc che no ai capît. Al è dificil intindisi cul inglês, se no tu i dâs la juste ghenghe. Cuissà dulà che a puartin i clients. Tal ostel al sarès convenient, magari intun YMCA, ven a stâi, associazion cristiane par mascjos. Pes zovinis si cumbine a presit. Naturalmentri twin beds, ancje la etichete e à la sô impuartance.
Ffrrr Ffrrr… Demoni cjalìn!! Il telefonut su la modalitât vibrazion. Dulà isal lât a finîle? Tal russac là jù insom dal jet. Sta a viodi che e je Carmela che mi clame sul celulâr. Shit! Mi soi dismenteât di telefonâi in Friûl.
Coventavie!? Culì dut ben, la sistemazion, la compagnie, pâs e ben, propit cumò e veve di telefonâ che i doi larons, sot e parsore, a stavin durmint. Se o ves di butâ jù dal jet un dai doi, o butarès jù il puçon disot, danât pe eternitât, ma cun cheste gjernazie al è miôr lassâ stâ, a Diu il Judizi Finâl.
Par fortune che o ai za pront il messazut tal archivi. 'Dut ben.' Un clic e vie!
Ve! La bombe etiliche disot si è dismote, e dopo une sgnofrade vie di corse in bagn a butâ fûr la anime. Intant che si disvuede, viodìn dal telefonut. Velu ca! No je contente. E à ancje reson, ma tant? ... Prime, ce vegnistu a fâ a Londre? O ai tant cefâ, no tu sâs la lenghe, e indenant cun cheste ghenghe. Cumò, nancje un sms par dî dut ben, dulà che o soi e cun cui. Simpri chê ossession tal cjâf, cuissà cui che lu console usgnot? Champagne e cotillons, feminis a manete, Londre ve! A voltis e somee dute une

recite, une robe paraiar, la vision di alc cence fonde. Cussì, par dâ a intindi ch'e je inrabiade, ma di sigûr e cjate simpri alc ce fâ in compagnie, fûr o dentri cjase. Lis amiis no i mancjin e nancje cualchi amì, magari cussì no! E ricêf simpri tancj compliments di chei che a lavorin cun jê. Il diretôr da la dite al è un om perfet, no i mancje propit nuie, un biel om. Mi pizzica, mi stuzzica. Feminis! Mandìn chest sms, prime che al torni fûr il cjochele dal bagn. Velu ca! Par fortune che al duar disot, se no al è bon di copâsi par lâ sù fin parsore tal jet a cjistiel. L'esperience e serf a alc. Forsi lu varan scrit ancje tal regolament dal ostel. I jets a nivel di paviment par chei parsore i sessantecinc, pai cjochelis e v.i. cuntune piçule zonte di cinc sterlinis. A son chei che a van vie subit cuant che a son lis partidis di balon, o cuant che a rivin in visite chei ninins dai black blocs che a doprin i jets parsore par meti l'armament: macis, casco, fiondis e dut ce che al serf par fâ un pôc di casin, e dopo lâ in zîr a vantâsi. Forsi, chei a àn ancje un franc te sachete par paiâsi un bon albierc, une discrete bustute, o la cjarte dal papi.
Cuissà se al è cambiât alc di cuant che Pier Paolo Pasolini al diseve che a son simpri chei che a tirin sù un grant davoi, fîs da la borghesie siore, un pôc stufadiçs par no savê ce fâ, un pôc bastians contraris cuintri i paris che ur tegnin in cjalt i puescj miôr di farmacist, avocat, nodâr, la sigurazion, la agjenzie imobiliâr, la concessionarie e v. i. Fîs cjavestris, pronts però a jentrâ di gnûf tal sisteme cuant che ur conven. Forsi cumò inta chê schirie alì a son ancje miscliçâts ducj chei che a àn pierdût il lavôr, o chei che no lu àn mai vût, par no dî dute la sdrume di imigrâts clandestins, invisibii, ombris che a vivin cun nô. A matine ti dan une man a parcâ la machine, ti spietin fûr dal supermarcjât pal euro, al semafar par netâti i veris dal

automobil, ti sunin il campanel par venditi ce saio jo, e ti svein di gnot par dâti une cucade a la cjase. No, gracie. La prossime volte.

No si rive mai a capî ce ore che e je tal ostel a buinore, soredut a Londre, cuant che al è innulât, cui palaçs tacâts di altris palaçs. No si sa se al è inmò scûr rampit o se al à tacât a fâ dì. Nancje un tor par sintî a bati lis oris e i cuarts d'ore, di fâti vignî un gnervôs cuant che tu stâs par indurmidîti. I cjochelis che a berlin jù in strade no son un bon orloi. No àn mai voie di lâ a durmî, e se plens come caratei a son bogns di metisi sot dal barcon a cuistionâ, a porconâ, a cjantâ. Dut il mont '1 è une butilie, la vite dome un cluc, cuant che si svuede la butilie, di sigûr no vâl un caz.

Pspspsps … Oh, Signôr, isal il sbrissul di chel parsore che al piert? Si sta insumiant a vôs alte, o forsi, spiete … Al è come se al murmuiàs la lezion pe scuele. Interogazion di matematiche doman cun chê biade di prof. Ce cjalcjut! Cuissà parcè che cuasi dutis lis insegnantis di matematiche a son feminis. Al varès di jessi l'incontrari, cul lôr cerviel plui predisponût pes lenghis, fat plui che evident. Forsi lu fasin di proposit par confondi lis ideis dai fantats za avonde malsestadis.

Spspspspsp, Jesus, al sta preant. Al sarà un marochin che al scuen preâ cuant che si alce e al va amont soreli, e ancje prin di lâ a durmî. A Marrakesh a jerin ducj in moschee aes dîs, undis di sere, dome mascjos, lis feminis denant da la television o a gucjâ, prin di tirâsi sot da la plete, dulà che a san ben lôr cemût fâsi rispietâ. Mi domandi se si pues preâ tal jet o se bisugne fâlu sul tapet in direzion di soreli jevât. Viers la puarte? No soi tant sigûr. Al è ben sta cuzos, mai disturbâ un che al pree. Al è bon di copâti pe fede. Voie di paradîs, cun chê biele anime di Beatrice che e cognòs ben jê i bai plui antîcs.

In vuaite! Al à metût i pîts a pendolon fûr dal jet. Profumâts come chei dai pelegrins in Cena Domini cun Pape Francesc. Sono neris? No si pues dî tal scûr. Zovin, tal salt che al à petât jù di adalt, e une biele tressadure, come un corazîr in direzion dal bagn. Spiete che o controli la ore sul telefonut. Cuatri. Che noia, che barba, che barba, che noia! Nol passe mai il timp e no ai durmide lûs. Nol rive lusôr dal barcon. Simpri il stes clarôr rossastri daûr dai veris da la citât indurmidide. Citât ireâl. O cîr dibant un barlum di lûs tra i lamps di cualchi rare machine che e cor vie ta la gnot. Ce fadie a tirâ indenant! Cui rivial aromai a cjapâ sium? A pene che il marochin al torne fûr dal bagn, o cor dentri jo. Podarès fâ un zîr pai coridôrs e cirî un altri libar, tant, a cheste ore a son ducj a durmî. No ai voie di pierdimi pai labirints degradâts dal ostel, cence un fregul di lûs, o pûr fâ cualchi incuintri pôc plasevul. Cuissà se al torne o se al è lât a fâ cualchi comission pai dormitoris. Al è un ostel cence pretesis, ma si rive a tirâ sù alc distès, se un al sa dulà meti man. Nol torne, mi alci jo cun atenzion cirint di no meti i pîts parsore chel disot, alore sì che o sarès malmetût. Sperìn che si sedi un fregul pasât. Plancuç, prime un pît dopo chel altri, il paviment che al criche sot i pîts, la puarte che e ciule sui cancars e o soi difûr. Une spere di lûs da la puarte dal bagn in sfese e nissun dentri. Il misar bagn inglês cu la moquette cragnose, une grande vasche cence la doce dal timp da la regjine Vitorie e nancje un picjot pai vistîts, un rubinet pe aghe cjalde, un par chê frede, e o sfidi un cristian a lavâsi in chê cragne. Ce pretesis assurdis! No isal mighe l'Hotel Hilton, cun chês cuatri sterlinis che mi à dât il president da la associazion? Mandât dal Comitât pal Amlêt Furlan, firmât dal secretari.

MISSION SPECIÂL A LONDRE

Sentât sul water dal ostel Saint James di Earls Court, cualchi minût dopo lis cuatri di buinore, o pensavi a la mê strane mission a Londre, a cemût che la storie e jere tacade, za fa dôs setemanis.

'Par une comission speciâl,' dissal par telefon il president dal Comitât pal Amlêt Furlan.

Precari a vite, o soi lât di buride a cjatâlu tal so ufici di Codroip. Al à tacât subite cu lis sôs mignassis.

'Tu âs studiât … Cui miôr di te al cognòs la lenghe? Tu vâs a Londre a tabaiâ cun chest professôr universitari, Ben Brough. Cumò al è in pension. Al è stât il plui impuartant colaboradôr dal professôr Cecil Clough, l'eminent studiôs di Shakespeare, che dopo agns di ricercjis al à afermât che lis fonts da la tragjedie *Romeo e Juliete* no son di cirî inta la lote di dôs fameis da la citât di Verone, ma e je une storie dute furlane, sucedude tal contest da la rivolte contadine di joibe grasse dal vincjesiet di fevrâr dal mil cinccent e undis,' al spiegà il president.

'Mi impensi inmò dal discors dal professôr Clough,' al continuà. 'Ve chi. Ti fâs une fotocopie da la riviste *Il Ponte*.'

La riviste e ripuartave par intîr il discors dal professôr Clough. Mi soi metût sù i ocjai e o ai let sot vôs un tocut dal so intervent.

'La storie apassionade dai doi zovins inamorâts, Luigi da Porto, alias Romeo Montecchi, e Lucina Savorgnan, alias Juliete Capuleti, e je sucedude a Udin tal fevrâr dal mil cinccent e undis. I doi fantats si son cognossûts intune gnot teribile, une gnot di violence in Friûl, e si son inamorâts a prime viste. No tant dopo, Luigi al è stât ferît in bataie e abandonât dal so amôr. Però, lui no si dismenteà di Lucina e al decidè di scrivi une storie tenare che il gjeni di Shakespeare al à trasformât in alc di universâl.

In cualsisei puest ducj a cognossin Romeo e Juliete. Ducj a cognossin la opare mestre di chest tragjic amôr. In cualsisei puest ducj a cognossin Verone, la citât di chest amôr universâl, ma no san nuie di Udin, il puest dulà che la vere storie e je sucedude, e no san nuie dai doi furlans, Luigi e Lucina, vêrs protagoniscj da la tragjedie.'

Ma dopo, cheste facende no je lade cussì ben, parcè che i furlans a son buine int, e invezit dal marketing, invezit di tirâ fûr une teraçute in centri a Udin, cuntun plante di vît che si rimpine sù fin al prin plan, une biele scrite in grant stîl 'Casa Savorgnan, alias Capuleti,' i furlans a son stâts cuiets. A varessin podût clamâ i figurants di Palme, specialiscj in rievocazions storichis. E dal puiûl là sù, une biele fantate furlane e podeve declamâ Shakespeare: 'Ce impuartial il non di une persone? Ce che nô o clamìn rose, cuntun altri non e varès distès un profum delicât …' Dutis lis domeniis, subite dopo Messe Grande, da lis primis, bielis zornadis di vierte fin al festival di fin istât, Halloween pe gjernazie plui zovine, cuant che si podeve pensâ a un grant bal finâl, cun costums dal Cinccent e mascaris, striis, fantasimis a volontât, e di sigûr cjastinis e ribuele a gratis par ducj. Nol coventave un comitât par cheste pensade, ma parcè tirâ fûr chestis strambetâts? O sin furlans! Ce vegnino a rompi i tabars? O stin ben cussì. 'Guglielmo, tu ti domandarâs parcè che ti ai clamât culì,' al continuà il president. 'Ce che ti ai contât fin cumò al è il passât. Une storie cuasi colade in dismentie. La grande novitât di vuê e je la ricercje fate dal colaboradôr e amì dal professôr Cecil Clough su lis fonts da la plui grande tragjedie di Shakespeare, l'*Amlêt*.'

'Sì, ma ce jentrial Codroip cul *Amlêt* di Shakespeare?' i ai domandât simpri plui curiôs.

'Ce premure! Spiete che ti conti!' il president mi fasè cuintri alçant il braç cun fastidi. 'No propite Codroip, ma o ai une buine reson par pensâ a la piçule comunitât di Cjamìn al Tiliment. Cun di fat il professôr Ben Brough dal so ricovar di Londre al sosten cun provade documentazion che Shakespeare par scrivi l'*Amlêt* al à fat riferiment a Riçart Secont da Cjamìn, marchês di Trevîs, forsi copât di so fradi Guecelon tal mil tresinte e dodis,' dissal il president cun cressint entusiasim.

'No rivi a capî il colegament tra i marchês da Cjamìn te Etât di Mieç e la piçule comunitât di Cjamìn al Tiliment,' i ai fat notâ un tininin malfident.

'Tu âs reson, i da Cjamìn a jerin marchês di Trevîs, ma a vevin simpri smicjât di cjapâ dentri de lôr Marcje ancje il Patriarcjât di Aquilee. E Cjamìn, il plui biel paîs dal Friûl, al devi vê fat un grum di gole ai marchês trevisans. Se no, parcè clamâlu Cjamìn e no alc altri?'

Une vore content da la sô analisi il president mi si vicine, mi cjape pal braç, e, come par confidâmi un grant segret, mi murmuie intune orele.

'Il fat plui incuietant al è chel di Amlêt, nevôt dal vecjo mulinâr di Cjamìn. Ti impensistu? Al leve in zîr a dî che lui al jere un princip da la Cjasade dai da Cjamìn. Il princip maledet, al berghelave a fuart, ultin dissendent da la impuartante famee dai Siôrs da Cjamìn, te Etât di Mieç, gjernazie maludide, maglade da la colpe di Cain, l'omicidi di so fradi Abêl.'

Cuant che il president al ve iniment Amlêt, no mi impensavi plui di lui, lu vevi dal dut dismenteât. Sparît za fa doi agns, muart al dîs cualchidun, forsi cussì mat nol

jere cuant che al leve tes ostariis a contâ che lui al jere un princip. Ducj in paîs lu coionavin cuant che al leve ator a mostrâ il sigjil da la famee dai da Cjamìn, un anel d'arint, blason dai Marchês di Trevîs, cjatât cuissà indulà. I ridevin daûr e lu clamavin 'biel princip', cun dispresi. I paiavin di bevi tes ostariis par viodilu çavariâ. 'Alc 'l è lât frait te Patrie dal Friûl,' al berghelave cuant che al jere cjoc disfat. Puar zovin, mi impensi che al è stât a lezion ancje chi di me, simpri cu la fissazion che la int no lu tratave cul rispiet che i spiete a un princip. Colât inmò di plui te depression, al à continuât a bevi e, dopo doi ricovars in ospedâl cul fiât in cirosi, al è sparît tal nuie. Al è lât ta la patrie dai siei vons, a murî sot lis ruvinis dal cjistiel dai marchês trevisans, inneât tal flum Sile e sparît par simpri, a àn continuât a dî par un pôc i cjaminês cuntun pocje di scuele. Fin cuant che il professôr Brough al à tirât fûr cheste prove sul *Amlêt* di Shakespeare. Ise une fissazion di un vieli studiôs, o pûr Shakespeare vevial plui a cûr il Friûl dai stes furlans che a disin in zîr che la lenghe furlane no conte un caz, e che covente savê dome l'inglês? 'Dôs coincidencis a fasin un indizi,' dissal il president. 'A chest pont, nô dal comitât no podevin tirâsi indaûr, parcè che la cuistion e podeve jessi une grande ocasion di promozion dal teritori. Dopo une riunion, la assemblee mi à incaricât di ocupâmi dal câs, e di viodi ce che al pensave il professôr Brough.'
Cuant che la notizie e je deventade publiche, si pues imagjinâ il gjalinâr che al è sucedût te piçule comunitât di Cjamìn, no dome tai bars e par strade, ma ancje sui social, sul gjornâl *Il Messaggero* e par television. I plui informâts a àn subite speculât che 'Elsinore', il puest dulà che si cjatave il cjistiel di *Amlêt* inta la tragjedie di Shakespeare, nol podeve che jessi tra i paîs di Stracis e Bugnins,

almancul cheste e jere la opinion dal Bar Sport. Ma i plui studiâts a àn tirât fûr il latin, 'Elsinore buscus ut extensa Varamus usque ad Tilimentum,' parcè che a sostignivin che Shakespeare al jere sì stravagant, ma distès nol podeve ambientâ la sô plui impuartante tragjedie a Stracis o Bugnins, se no cuissà ce cjatadis che i grancj mestris di toponomastiche furlane a varessin tiradis fûr tes lôr cunvignis.

Dopo vê acetât la idee di vignî in Ingletiere a tabaiâ cul professôr Brough, e vê fissât ducj i detais, o stevi par lâ vie cuant che il president mi ven dongje e mi met une man su la spale.

'In confidence, i dîs une robe che no varès di dî a dinissun, segret professionâl,' al murmuià. 'Il maressial dai carabinîrs mi à pandût che a stavin investigant cul carbonio cutuardis!'

E dopo al platà la bocje cuntune man e mi disè planc inta la orele:

'A àn cjatât dai vues di cristian inviluçâts tal cellophane sot dal supermarcjât Cadoro, cuntune scrite in grant, HAM! Putane Eve! Amlêt par inglês si scrîf Hamlet, nomo?'

'Sigûr.'

'Dôs coincidencis a fasin un indizi, trê coincidencis a fasin une prove. Guglielmo, cor vie a Londre che dopo ti din un puest fis di vice president dal Comitât!'

No ai olsât a dî nuie al puar om, che al podeve jessi un prossut di San Denêl pal export, frait patoc, metût intun sac par che nol snorbei, e dopo dismenteât par future memorie. O ai simpri considerât l'ignorance une pome esotiche tant delicade che a pene tu le tocjis la floridure s'int va.

Tornâ dal bagn al dormitori al è come saltâ fûr dal labirint di Cnosso cence il fîl di Ariane. A drete, a çampe, no si capìs mai dulà zirâ, e se e fos un pocje di lûs di viodi i numars ... Mancjarès ancje cheste cumò di domandâ aiût. Finalmentri, velu ca il numar vincjeun, e se al è il vincjeun, al scuen jessi ancje il vincjecinc. Avanti Savoia! Ve ce che a servissin i cors di orienteering, prime dì di scuele aes superiôrs.

Mi somee di viodi un pocje di lûs che e rive difûr. Al comence a fâ dì. No ai nissune voie di provâ a durmî inta chel cjôt. O voi dentri cidin, cidin par cjoli i vistîts, e vie pe citât, libar di esisti.

Vincjecinc. Viodìn se il pomul al zire di podê vierzi la puarte. Un odôr di no rivâ a respirâ, e no son zîs! Par no murî intosseât in chel efluvi, o grampi a la svelte une felpe, i jeans, il russac cu lis cjartis e i bêçs vanzâts, se no mai àn za netâts, come mi jere sucedût di frut te colonie di Fratis, in montagne. Al sparive simpri dut dai dormitoris, e se tu contavis aes assistentis, ti jemplavin di botis chei bulos di Torrimpietra. Ce bulisim! Ti drecin la schene, ti judin a cressi, tu viodarâs sot la naie! Cussì ti confuartavin i esperts educatôrs dal neolitic furlan. Mi vevin fin robât la dutrine che mi jeri puartât di cjase par ripassâ chês nozions cragnosis. Disgracie da la famee, fin rimandât in dutrine chel an infeliç. Dove è Dio? A guardare della mia bici che non me la rubino, ve! Ma ce che al jere piês, mi vevin fin taconât lis figurinis dal Milan, cun Gianni Rivera, l'abatino, e Pierino Prati, la peste. O vevi propite vaiût di cûr par la pierdite, la robe plui cjare che o vevi. Prime di partî par Fratis, mê mari e leve a comprâ lis cartulinis e i boi di spedî cu lis buinis gnovis da la colonie.

'Parcè no mi scrivistu dôs riis tu cumò, cussì dopo jo o ai dome l'intric di spedîlis?' i sugjerivi.

'Ma ce ti scrivio?' mi domandave une vore maraveade.

'Che o stoi ben, che o mangji e che o ai fin metûts sù doi chilos.'
Situazion che no si è mai verificade, anzit, cu la sorprese da lis assistentis, jo o tornavi a cjase inmò plui sec candît. Però no jeri l'unic che par stress e avilizion al pative in chel lager. Un gno compagn di vot agns al jere fin scjampât di chel puest misar, e si jere metût a cori dilunc la Pontebane, fin a Dogne. Lu àn cjatât che al vaive disperât, sentât suntune piere a ôr da la strade. Dopo vêlu pacât di vueli sant, lu àn spedît a cjase cu la prime coriere.
Al è tornât da la ronde ancje il marochin parsore che mi spie. Mi fâs fin sens, puar Crist, al pensarà dulà vaial a finî chel soci alì cu la citât inmò invuluçade tal scûr? E cumò vie in esplorazion di Londre cence il trafic e la confusion da la ore di ponte.
La impleade a la reception mi da une cjalade di stoz.
'Bundì. Di dulà diaul …?' mi domande secjade.
'Dormitori vincjecinc.'
Une cjalade aes cjartis.
'Guglielmo?'
'Sì. Soi jo.'
'Okay.' E in silenzi par no fâsi sintî. 'Sboràts di talians. Mai che a stedin tal lôr puest!'
Al covente capî ce che ti domandin, e no fâ come gno cugnât a la sigurece dal aeropuart JFK. Lu àn tignût dentri une ore, la piês da la sô vite, parcè che nol rivave a spiegâ a un bocon di poliziot abronzât, voi triscj, ce che al faseve a New York e dulà che al veve prenotât di durmî.

BUINORE A HYDE PARK

Fûr al comence a sclarî. Mancumâl! O pues passâ par un che al va a vore cuntun pas svelt, se no tal scûr lis animis invisibilis da la gnot ti fermin a ogni crosade, e al è un pericul a voltâur lis spalis e fâ fente di nuie. Salacor tu ti intivis tal bastart che al tire fûr un curtìs. 'O ai di mangjâ ancje jo e i fruts piçui, la femine plene e la none in carozele.' Al covente simpri tignî pront un biliet di dîs sterlinis, o cincuante se nol baste.

Nissun al rive a imagjinâ trop biel che al è torzeonâ par Londre sul cricâ dal dì intune biele zornade di istât. Dome cualchi rare machine e passe di buride dilunc i larcs boulevarts dal centri, ma pes viutis plui scuindudis nol è nissun in zîr. Cualchi vecjut mi cjale dal barcon a pene spalancât, un sbîr mi à olmât a une cierte distance, mi ten di voli su dulà che o voi. O scuen acelerâ il pas, fâ viodi che no ai brutis intenzions, che une reson par lâ ator par Londre cussì a buinore le ai, e no voltâmi a cjalâlu. A son lôr a controlâ e no l'incontrari.

A son lis cinc di buinore, il dîs di avost a Londre. Juste une bavisele frescje, ma si sta ben difûr cuant che no si rive a durmî. Al è come ripiâsi, tornâ a vivi, tu ringraciis Diu di jessi nassût, tu ti sintis plui bon e tu volaressis fâ alc par chest mondat malsestât. Hyde Park al pues jessi il puest ideâl par rivâ di buinore a passâ la ore, prime da la gulizion.

Pal cuartîr di Kensington e je la vie plui curte par rivâ tal parc. Mi intivi in tantis piçulis covis, ripârs pe gnot, bars, puescj par gjoldi un fregul di cheste vitace. Une cjoche, un sbal par meti un tacon al vueit che o vin dentri. Int strane che si pindule fûr e dentri dal locâl, stracs pe baldorie da la gnot, un miscliç di gjernazie umane. Da la putane cul ultin spagnolet, lungjis gjambis in pose sensuâl su la sente zirevule denant dal banc, che mi cjale cun voi sturnîts, a la int indurmidide sul divan daûr, a altris di lôr cul cjâf puntelât sul comedon poiât al banc, voi che mi fissin cence viodimi. Dut li dentri ti da un sens di sporc, pôc curât, e dilunc viâl difûr intun grant bacan a vegnin indenant siet, vot di lôr daûr dal camion da la netece urbane. A tirin sù la cragne da la gnot che e à cuasi dal dut lassât il puest al gnûf dì.

Hyde Park al somee jessi un puest fûr dal mont. Dute la nature e gjolt te pâs di prime matine. Te Serpentine, il lât al centri dal parc, une file di razutis si corin daûr, e il gorghisâ di un mierli mi da l'impression di jessi di bessôl in chest mont. Londre. Lis pocjis personis che mi capite di incrosâ mi saludin, mi fasin muse di ridi, cuntun moviment dal cjâf di condivision. Cuant che il prin soreli al cuche fûr da la fumadice, mi ven voie di tornâ frut, di cori daûr da la sghirate che si met devant par dispiet, o l'ucielut che mi schive par un pêl pe presse di puartâ il mangjâ ai picinins.

Dute la grande citât e somee vistîsi da la bielece da la albe. Lis cjasis tal cuartîr di Belgravia a somein indurmididis, e i palaçs si impiin luminôs, splendents, tal cîl pûr, cristalin da la matine. Dut al lusìs intal aiar cence smog.

Mi senti suntune bancjine cul desideri che chest moment nol finissi plui, che al duri par simpri, ma il cûr potent da la citât al è li in spiete di partî di gnûf. Di moment in moment dut al sarà diferent. No ai voie di alçâmi plui di culì, mi si sierin i voi da la sium. O ai voie di durmî, voie di murî cussì intune biele matine di istât a Londre.

La cjampane da la Glesie da la Inmaculade, viers Piccadilly, e sune l'Ave Marie. Il sun al rive di lontan cu la citât che si sta sveant. Nol è un insium, a son lis sîs di buinore a Londre.

MATINE A CJAMIN

I glons da la Ave Marie si spandin pe campagne di Cjamìn
al Tiliment cuant che Carmela e torne a cjase. Nol è nissun
a spietâle. Si cjale tal spieli dal bagn: la muse tirade, cence
espression, i voi piçui e stracs. Dut al mostre la cjame dai
agns, ma al è miôr no pensâ, e cuntune biele durmide dut
al tornarà compagn. Cui rivie adore a cjapâ sium cumò,
dopo une serade cussì, passade cul miò amât diretôr? Nol
voleve propit lassâmi lâ vie. Mi rive di daûr, dut
imboreçât, intant che o stavi finint un lavôr al computer.
Mi poie une man su la spale e me cjarece cun delicatece.
Dongje da la cincuantine, la stesse etât di Guglielmo, ma
dut un altri snait, une altre passion. A proposit, spiete che o
viôt se mi à scrit un sms di Londre chel puar biât dal gno
om. 'Dut ben.' Di sigûr no si romp i tabars a scrivi di plui
o a clamâmi. Al è tal so caratar. Miôr cussì, al vîf plui a
lunc lui, e al lasse vivi ancje me. O soi masse strache par
la preiere. Magari un Atto di Dolore, mi pento, mi dolgo ...
Par fortune che doman no si va a vore, si passe la ore a fâ
l'amôr. Ben dite.
Mi stevi preparant par lâ a cjase. Al jentre cidin tal gno
ufici e al siere la puarte daûrsi.
'Carmela, avrei qualcosa di importante da dirti sulla
prossima fiera.' Di colp al met lis mans sui miei flancs. Mi
tire viers di se cuntun ridi lusorôs. Daspò mi busse cun
passion. Jo, un sgrisul in dut il cuarp, o ai pierdût il
sintiment. No ai resistût al gno cjâr diretôr, al putanîr dal
gno diretôr. Mi impensi cuant ch'e je stade la prime volte.
O jeri in prime medie tal convit des muiniis. O vevi ripetût
la classe chel an. Lui si clamave Pauli e al faseve la tierce.
Chê primevere o rivavin simpri a scjampâ fûr dopomisdì, e

o levin par cjamps daûr dal convit, a cirî un puest cidin. Al è sucedût dut cussì a la svelte. Jo sot e lui parsore. Lis sôs mans a esploravin dut il gno cuarp. Mal soi tirât strent parsore di no capî plui nuie. Mi à slargjadis lis gjambutis, mandi oh mê vergjinitât.

Cence gjenitôrs fin di picinine, tal convit un ciert morbin mi cresseve dentri ancje cu lis muiniis. Mi clamavin Shirley Temple, no ai mai capît parcè, cuant che ur sculetavi denant sbatint il cjâf di ca e di là a ogni pas, dut un riçot biont. Mi plaseve ancje strenzimi intor des novizis, fâmi cjareçâ di lôr, e la gnot, prime di indurmidîmi, tra un Pateravegloria, par cuietâle mi bastave la manute. O ai lassât il convit a disevot agns cuant che mi soi metude cuntun sposât, su la cincuantine. Plen di bêçs, ma no tant ben di salût, e jo stupide e zovine o vevi ancje plasê a umiliâlu. Al è lât cun Gjo za fa cualchi an, puar om, e no rivi a parâmal vie dal cjâf che un pocje di colpe le ai vude ancje jo.

E dopo o ai cognossût Guglielmo. O ai scugnût fâ dut jo, figurâsi, mi cjalave di sot coç, timit. Si capive che i plasevi, sfidi jo, nol veve mai tocjât une femine! Disimi che tu mi vuelis ben, sì ti vuei ben e vie a bussâsi intal cine. A davin il film 'Malizie' cun Laura Antonelli. O jeri dute imboreçade. Un bon om, jal ai simpri dit, e di sigûr o soi convinte. I plui biei moments da la mê vite, par simpri, ti promet di jessiti fedêl fin a la fin, e di volêti ben e onorâti par ducj i dîs da la mê vite. Biâts oms! Al è cussì dificil il concet di famee in dì di vuê, di un rapuart che al dure dute une vite, di viodi se stes come part di une altre persone, une sô metât, o soi Heathcliff, ancjemò di plui par me che no soi mai rivade a condividi alc di impuartant cu lis personis che o ai cjatadis te vite. Simpri in lote, simpri ae ricercje di une rivincite personâl. Cumò ti fâs viodi jo, ninin! Guglielmo mi à dât une grande man al inizi. Mi cjapave pal cûl, e mi clamave la sô sex bomb, ma dopo al à come capît che jo i cjapavi dut il spazi, che dut al deventave routine. Nol à di sigûr zovât il gno ategjament agressîf viers i oms. La Belle Dame sans merci ti ten sclâf. E dopo e je stade la pierdite di nestri fi. Un dolôr che o cîr simpri di platâ. Cumò mi dîs: 'O scuen lâ a Londre par tabaiâ cuntun professôr. No pues puartâ ancje te. E vignarà ben une altre ocasion.' Po ben, e jo o voi cul diretôr, plui par fastidi che desideri di svindic, une voie istintive di tornâ a la vite mâl sablassade di prime, cence une moralitât dissiplinade, cence regulis di rispietâ.

Lui al è tornât a vivi la sô vite di single, tant cefâ mi dîs, cuant che al torne a cjase rabiôs cui coleghis. E dopo si siere tal salot a viodi la television di bessôl. Ce fasie une femine come me cuntun om cussì? Dome cualchi incroci cu la mê vite, un jet frêt, dopo che o vin pierdût il nestri fantulin. Za fa dîs agns, aromai. Une vite. Lu spietavi chel fi come un don di Diu, e mi someave di vivi la realtât di cualchidune altre, come se une lûs mi ves invuluçade e mi compagnàs viers un destin discognossût. Mi sintivi plui buine. A jerin bielis zornadis di vierte cu la nature in amôr, e ancje jo mi sintivi part di chel cambiament ta la vite di ognidun, chel passaç che une nassite e rive a evocâ. Dutis lis personis a vevin une atenzion particolâr viers di me. Di sigûr, in chestis situazions une femine e je di bessole, e dome cul caratar e cu la fuarce che o vin dentri si rive a puartâsi fûr. L'impression che o podès cambiâ vite, che al fos pussibil dismenteâ il passât e tornâ a partî. Cumò a distance di dîs agns dut al è tornât compagn di prime. Il sgurli al zire, al zire par tornâ al pont di partence. Il passât al è simpri cun me, mi sburte indaûr ai agns di frute, a la malizie che ti jude a frontâ il mont carogne che si cjatìn

denant. No sarès mai rivade, e no rivararès mai a la disperazion da la puarete che e jere dongje di me tal ospedâl. No finive plui di vaî. O pensi che e vignìs da la Colombie, ma no soi tant sigure. O stoi par separâmi dal gno om, mi conte. O savevi che nol varès funzionât, o sin cussì diferents. E jere une sensazion, mal sintivi dentri. L'an passât o ai pierdût il frut, Marco, incinte di cinc mês. La puarete e vaive di cûr ancje vie pe gnot. O volevi chel frut. O vevi bisugne di Marco. Mi àn dit che al jere un virus cjapât cuissà indulà in zîr pal mont. Cumò, culì in ospedâl, o ai pierdût il frut une altre volte, doi mês. Puare femine! Al è dificil imagjinâ la vite di chei puarets che a rivin chi di nô, cu la sperance di podê començâ alc di impuartant. Dopo, la delusion. Il gno om si sint in trapule, malcontent. Al vûl tornâ in Colombie. Al à provât cetancj lavôrs, ma nol rive a restâ intun puest. Lis tantis oris di lavôr che un nol è usât par une paie di miserie, che no tu rivis nancje a comprâti il mangjâ. E cumò o stin par separâsi. Noooo! No vuei tornâ in Colombie cun lui. No sai se i vuei ancjemò ben, si confidave cun me ogni sere tal ospedâl, vaint di no dâsi pâs. O ai di cjatâ un lavôr culì. O scuen cjatâ un lavôr par paiâmi l'afit. Al è masse cjâr, ma no pues tornâ cjase dai miei in Colombie. Mi sbataressin la puarte in muse, o soi sigure. Tu varessis di stâ a sintî ce che ti disin i gjenitôrs. Ti cognossin miôr di cualsisei altri. O volevi cussì tant chest frut, Marco. Ce mi sucedial? No sai plui ce fâ. Puare me! Puare me!
A son lis vot di matine cuant che Carmela e cjape sium.

L'INCUINTRI CUN HORATIO

A son lis sîs di buinore a Londre. O soi sentât suntune bancjine a Hyde Park, intune biele matinade frescje di istât. Denant di me, a meridion, la magnifiche viodude dal Royal Albert Hall che al sflandore te lûs dal prin soreli. Mi si vicine un siorut.

'Puedio …?'

'Comodaitsi!' Lu invidi a sentâsi.

Su la sessantine, magri, moviments svelts, gnervôs, ben barbirât, luncs cjavei grîs leâts daûr cuntun codin, une cjamese a cuadris che i sbalote fûr dai jeans a rimarcâ il so fisic sclagn. Al cjacare un inglês perfet, e cuant che i conti che o soi talian, al cîr di improvisâ cualchi frase cu la sô cognossince dal spagnûl, da la sô vite passade in Messico a insegnâ inglês. Mi conte dal bon mangjâ di chel paîs, da lis dîs regulis di vite par evitâ il stress, dal parcè che o sin li aes sîs di buinore a passâ la ore. Mi ven di pensâ che al è un om di bessôl, che ancje jo o soi di bessôl. E tancj di lôr mi cjalin in muse, e mi fermin par strade par domandâ une informazion, un plasê, e magari mi fasin ancje une confidence, come cuant che tu sês a cjaminâ in montagne e tu volaressis contâ dute la tô vite a une persone che tu âs a pene cognossût. E sarà cuestion di voi che a cjalin, voi bogns che a cirin di capî, che a contemplin maraveâts la realtât. Ciertis personis a àn scrit sul cerneli, jo o soi fat par comandâ, e no stait a rompi i tabars parcè che no ai timp di pierdi, e dopo a son lis personis cence cualitâts, cussì lis clamin, simpri prontis a dâ une man, che si cirin te bisugne.

Mi conte che ancje lui al vîf intun ostel, tal Phoenix Hostel, dongje Regent's Park, dulà che al cognòs il paron che i da la stanzie e il mangjâ a gratis par cualchi ore di lavôr come receptionist.

Ancje jo tra cualchi an come chest sioret culì, cence patrie, cence afiets, di bessôl pal mont. Situazion che mi fâs cuasi gole, mi fâs pensâ a la nestre condizion di umign, cun plui onestât viers nô stes, a ce che o stin a fâ culì di bessôi, a sintî dute la confusion che nus contorne, la falsetât, i cocodecs di cheste gjernazie umane. Disìn vonde a ducj i dîs te coruzion, falsetâts, peteçs!

Dopo vê tant tabaiât di se, mi domande cui che o soi, se o fâs alc di sest te vite.

'Sì, o soi un studiôs,' i dîs.

Un libar professionist, un ricercjadôr, un cerviel in fughe. Nol è facil fâsi capî tal forest cuant che si cjacare di Italie. Cemût rivistu a spiegâi che tu sês un precari da la scuele a cuasi cincuante agns, che tu lavoris un pôc chi, un pôc là, che cumò a Londre tu sês in mission par la cagade di un comitât grotesc, e pe vision di un puar vecjo professôr in pension? Robe di mats!

'O ai capît, e … cuale ise la sô impuartante mission culì a Londre?' mi domande.

Sigûr, une mission par cont di Diu. Ce bale i contio cumò? No soi mighe John Belushi. E parcè no dîsi la veretât? Ancje une veretât intrigose, paradossâl, ridicule, e pues pandi alc di impuartant su la nature umane, il pavonâsi in sene par une ore prime dal grant cidinôr.

I spieghi da la ricercje su lis fonts dal teatri di Shakespeare.

'Shakespeare? La mê passion, il gno amôr, il gno dut!' il siôr al proclame in estasi.

L'entusiasim dal omenut mi sburtin a contâi di *Romeo e Juliete*, di *Amlêt*, ma al è dome un piçul interval, parcè che mi sucêt dispès di cjatâ simpri cualchidun che mi sburte in bande, che al monte in scagn, e la mê idee, il gno progjet al devente inconsistent, fin a sparî dal dut, par lassâ il puest a la sapience di chei che a àn simpri une rispueste, che a àn clâr denant di se dulà che a stan lant, o pûr semplicementri a àn voie di jemplâ un vueit, e si movin svelts intun mont di ombris. Ma chest siorut achì al sa veramentri alc di *Amlêt*, nol è come il nestri cicciobombo cannoniere politic, che pûr di fâ viodi trop brâf che al è, al riscje ancje cualchi frase par inglês. De, de, de … Mi conte che al à recitât Shakespeare fin di picinin, lu à simpri doprât tes sôs classis.

'Mercutio e je stade la mê ultime part di atôr,' mi conte e al cite un frase dal *Romeo e Juliete*.

'O cjacari di siums, che a son fîs di un cerviel indolent, creâts dome di fantasiis svoladiis.'

'Recitial ancjemò?' i domandi.

'No plui.' Dopo chê ultime audizion i àn dite che al jere masse vecjo, che a cirivin cualchidun plui zovin.

'Obsolêt. Magari a vevin ancje reson,' mi dîs.

Ma cemût rassegnâsi al fat che un al pense di vê dentri di se ancjemò tant ce dâ? E forsi al pues vê ancje reson, parcè che chei che a sburtin par jentrâ no àn di sigûr la sô cognossince, la sô esperience. No lu dîs, forsi, nancje lu pense. Si ferme un moment di tabaiâ e mi cjale fis tai voi, come par viodi se o spartìs la sô opinion.

'Pensial cussì ancje lui?' mi domande.

Forsi esperience e cognossince a son stupidagjinis intun mont che al cor masse a la svelte. Ce tip di esperience e cognossince puedial vê un om che al jere zovin plui di cincuante agns indaûr, cuant che i valôrs a jerin cetant diferents? Dome opinions svoladiis. E pûr intun mont cu la popolazion che e devente simpri plui vecje, al covente cjatâ une soluzion par evitâ un conflit tra gjenerazions. Ce colpe aial un anzian di deventâ vecjo? Il vôt grîs, il dirit di lâ a votâ par chei che a àn i cjavei grîs, e a vivin masse a lunc. La publiche opinion e pense che il mont al è cambiât, e lôr vecjos no àn il dirit di decidi par chei plui zovins. Par chei che a zirin il mont, cerviei in fughe, come uciei di pas che a svolin libars, cence la fuarce di gravitât, e a aterin dulà che il lôr estri ju vuide. A àn cun lôr il navigadôr satelitâr par la strade plui curte, chê mancul traficade, chê dulà che no si paie il dazi.

Tancj di lôr a stan a cjase, cence lavôr, cun pôcs bêçs te sachete, juste ce che ur passe il papi. Il nestri Gri pentastelât, comic timp indaûr, cumò al fâs ridi par so cont, al volarès ben passâ une leç su la 'rotamazion' dai anzians, e in Ingletiere a son tornâts a lis teoriis di Malthus, za fa dusinte agns. Par lui lis epidemiis a jerin la gracie di Diu par contignî la cressite da la popolazion. In linie cun Malthus tancj inglês a pensin che par fâ cuintri a lis pandemiis bisugne rivâ a la inmunitât dal trop, cul risultât che a inmalâsi e sparî di chest mont a son i plui debii, i anzians. No stin nancje contâ i todescs che a àn simpri rimedis estrems. No vino mighe di gasâju chescj puars vecjos! Ce colpe àno se a vivin plui a lunc, cul reminder da lis midisinis che al sune ogni ore? La pirule pal cûr, chê par la pression, par sintî ben, par viodi miôr, par resurî il desideri, e magari ancje la pastiliute pes nonis che a vuelin fâ fîs a sessante, cumò che o vin la crisi demografiche.

Il vêr probleme a saressin lis pensions: no varessin avonde bêçs par ducj. Si podarès stampâju i bêçs, ma se nol è nuie ce mangjâ, ce ti servino? Bisugnarès inventâ des punturis che ti fasin passâ la fan. I miedis a disin che i vecjos a àn di mangjâ ben: strachin e tante verdure di stagjon, e bevi tante buine aghe minerâl, almancul doi litris in dì, che ti fâs pissâ, e mangjâ pomis, bananis soredut, e une taçute di bon vin neri a past. Masse pretesis i vecjuts! No si cumbine. Al covente fâ un pat cul Pari Eterni. Nô i mandìn i vecjuts plui clopadiçs e chei parsore i setante. A chei al pense Lui. Ur da di mangjâ e ancje alc cefâ, parcè che no si sta ben cence fâ nuie. Robis di pôc s'intint. Ce saio jo? Se in chest mont al jere un bon eletricist, al podarès controlâ la luminarie dal Paradîs, se al jere un eletricist trist, al podarès fâ un fregul di manutenzion dai condizionadôrs dal Infier. Se invezit al jere un bon casâr, al podarès fâ il formadi light che al jude la levitazion, se al jere un casâr trist, al podarès fâ il formadi cui viers, e ogni tant butâ sù sul fûc sot lis cjalderiis. Se al jere un cogo trist, al podarès fâ risot cui foncs velenôs, se invezit al jere un sant cogo, al podarès fâ dome robis buinis che tant in Paradîs no si riscje di ingrassâ. Però, forsi ancje il Pari Eterni nol sarès tant content di vê dome vecjuts, e al volarès ancje cualchi cristiane, zovinute di prin pêl. E daspò, o ai pôre che nol à masse puest nancje lui là sù. I cinês e i indians i àn simpri dât problemis, cence contâ che al è inmò daûr a sistemâ chei che a àn fat fûr i todescs. No stin contâ chei che a son stâts fiscâts dai comuniscj, tant chei no ju cjate nissun. Cuissà, a varan cjatât il sisteme par reincjarnâsi parcè che di lôr nissun al cjacare, nissun al scrîf.

La mê gnove cognossince e à fermât a colp di tabaiâ. Forsi al varà capît che no i stavi plui daûr, jentrât tal gno mont segret, tal mont paralêl, il mâr infinît li che mi plâs pierdimi. Dolce il naufragar in questo mare. Al à di sigûr intuît di vêmi robât il gno spazi. Nol sucêt tant dispès te realtât di ogni dì di cjatâ personis cussì sensibilis. Par solit, e je une corse sbrenade indenant par fâ viodi trop brâfs che o sin, ce inteligjence superiôr che nus à dât il Pari Eterni!

No, nol à di ce scusâsi. O sin culì in chest mont par cirî di
lassâ un segn, magari dome un flevar ricuart, une
memorie, par no vignî dismenteâts. E o tornìn simpri ai
moments plui biei da la nestre vite, cuant che o crodevin a
alc di veramentri impuartant, e nus plâs viviju di gnûf chei
moments, ancje un pôc plui biei te nestre imagjinazion,
forsi esaltâts fin a une aureole di santitât.
Ce biele cheste trancuilitât a Hyde Park, cuant che dôs
personis si inacuarzin che alc di impuartant al sta par
començâ.
L'orloi dal tor di Picadilly al bat lis siet, e jo o capìs che
chest professôr in pension, chest ex-atôr di Shakespeare,
mi acompagnarà tal gno viaç a Londre ae ricercje dal
professôr Brough, e ae scuvierte dal misteri dal Amlêt
furlan.
'Mi clami Horatio,' si presente cence cerimoniis par ripiâ
la conversazion.
'O soi Guglielmo. O ai plasê di cognossilu!'
'Ancje jo. Feliç di fâ la sô cognossince,' cuntune
energjiche strete di man par condividi il moment speciâl
che o stin vivint.
Horatio, come l'amì di *Amlêt* ta la tragjedie
Shakespeariane, il prin a viodi la fantasime dal vecjo re,
'se tu âs un cualchi sunôr, o ûs da la vôs, fevele …'
Personaç ideâl par metisi in contat cul mont di là.
Sul vignî gnot, a torzeon dilunc la roste fûr di Cjamìn al
Tiliment, cuntune fumate penze che si taie cul curtìs, fin a
la cjase dirocade dal vecjo mulinâr, nono di Amlêt, il zovin
lât vie di bintar, sparît za fa doi agns e mai plui tornât. La
cuestion e sta deventant ingredeade, invuluçade intun
mont di misteri, un vencul che al torne sù cu lis ombris da
la gnot.
Horatio mi fâs sintî mancul di bessôl te mission culì a

Londre. Al à insegnât inglês in dut il mont, e cumò al è tornât a cjase, ae citât da la sô zoventût. Plen di ricuarts, ma ancje siôr dentri par continuâ il so percors di vite, cirint di condividi alc cu lis animis libaris, spirts bintars come lui che no rivin a stâ fers intun puest, che no si lassin cjapâ dentri il maljessi dal mont, no si preocupin dal dispresi dal timp che al passe cussì a la svelte, vecjos cence acuarzisi, meteoris che a van a murî lontan. Quia pulvis es, et in pulverem reverteris, cuntune piçade di cinise sui cjavei.

Mi imagjini Horatio di zovin ator pal mont, Shakespeare scjampât di Stratford-upon-Avon, da la femine, dai fîs, dai afiets plui cjârs, libar di esisti, simpri a complicâsi la esistence daûr a situazions ingredeadis, invezit di cirî di gjoldi des robis semplicis che la vite nus risierve. Horatio nol sarà come lis personis che a aspirin a cambiâti la vite, a salvâti dal mâl par puartâti viers il ben. O compri la tô anime, le salvi dai pinsîrs neris … e le consegni a Diu. Ma distès lu stimi come une persone che ti pues judâ a cjatâ speris di lûs, passâ moments serens che magari par cualchi atim ti fasin gjoldi la vite, scuvierzi un sens plui profont. La sô vite, la nestre vite, insioradis di tantis storiis comunis, di robis lontanis, dolôrs antîcs che a son stâts e a puedin tornâ di gnûf.

Al è une vore incuriosît dal studi dal professôr Brough sul *Amlêt* di Shakespeare, e cuant che i conti che al è ospit di cheste cjase di ricovar, Forrester Court Care Home, dongje a Paddington, mi dîs di colp:

'O sai dulà che si cjate.'

Mal viôt chest bonom che al zire par Londre a pît, chilometris e chilometris, par intopâsi in personis sbandadis come me, e cun ognidune al cîr la reson dal parcè di cheste volontât imanent che nus ten atîfs, plens di progjets, ancje di vecjos, simpri cu la sperance di rivâ a lassâ alc daûr, magari dome un segn che nus fasi dî o jeri, o ai fat, o conti alc, no ai vivût par nuie.

Horatio mi spieghe ben che no sin lontans, e dopo cuatri pas dilunc Hyde Park, a traviers i zardins di Kensington, si rive su la Queensway, dulà che a son tancj puestuts par mangjâ une bocjade a presit. E insom da la vie, daûr la stazion dai trens di Paddington, si rive tal ospizi. Cheste aventure lu incuriosìs, soredut in gracie di Shakespeare, par sintî di un professôr alc di diferent su chest grant om. Un studi che nol sedi come i peteçs dai gjornâi che a scrivin che il novante par cent dai inglês al cognòs i titui di dome dôs des sôs oparis, o che lu ritegnin contemporanii, o che al è un gay, un da la gjenerazion beat, o altris stupidagjinis che a provin che la mari dai dordui e je simpri plene, che la ignorance e je une fuarce di no crodi … tocjile e la floridure s'int va.

A son lis siet e mieze di matine cun za tante int in zîr. La grande metropoli e je tal davoi da la ore di ponte. Londre e je speciâl intune biele matinade di soreli estîf. Un miscliç di int che e cjamine di buride dilunc Queensway, vie cosmopolite, une sdrume di ristorants, soredut orientâls, cafès e piçui negozis, pachistans, indians, supermarcjâts 24/7. La parone a la casse e il paron su la puarte par controlâ che i clients no scjampin cence paiâ. Si cjate la robe a presit, no je la voie di profitâ. Tant chei li a son di passaç, cui ju viôt plui? E la lôr comunitât e cres, si svilupe, simpri pronts a dâsi une man. Un mont di sacrificis che nô furlans o vin dismenteât di dopo incà. No capìn plui dulà che chel cristian, musulman, o ce saio jo, al cjate un fin, un obietîf, une reson di vite par tirâ indenant, content di ce che al rive a meti dongje dì par dì, content di stâ in chest mont, di jessi un esempli di onestât. Un grant insegnament pai fîs che a cressin protets intune famee cun valôrs impuartants. I bêçs, il benstâ ti dan cuntune man e ti cjolin cun chê altre, e un si sint plui puar dentri.

GULIZION TAL ENGLISH CAFÈ

Horatio al cjamine sigûr. Si capìs che al cognòs la zone come lis sôs sachetis. Al jentre intun locâl a la buine, a gjestion familiâr. Al salude la parone, une siore inglese sui sessante, une arie trascurade e stufadice, usade di agns ai stes clients, cui solits plats da la tradizion, cence pretesis. Lis tindinis da la vetrade sul esterni a àn cognossût la regjine Vitorie. Une puce di frit si spant pardute la sale, e une cragne cuasi naturâl, un sporc sedimentât, di robis fruiadis e vecjis si è poiât su dut l'ambient.

La parone e à doi voi di çuite, une cjalade severe, la espression che a àn i cjargnei cuant che a viodin un forest. Ce sêstu vignût a fâ ca sù, a rompi i tabars? Mi ven di pensâ che Horatio al podarès vê une brute reputazion in cont di paiâ. La siore mi olme cun suspiet. Stesse gjernazie, cence lavôr, cence bêçs e cence mangjâ. Se a cjolin alc cence paiâ, se viodin cul gno om che di sigûr no ju fâs lavâ i plats, ma al clame il sbîr. Il puest al è piçul cun cinc taulins cul plan in formiche, cence tavaie, cun cjadreis a la buine.

O sin dome nô doi. No vin timp di sentâsi che la parone nus met in man un cartoncin di plastiche cun scrit il menù de gulizion suntune bande e chel dal gustâ su chê altre. Par fortune ducj i plats a son a presit, un fastidi di mancul. Cumò al è di viodi cui che al paie par Horatio. Se mi met in cont il servizi di acompagnâmi par Londre, o soi taconât. Il plat plui economic al è l'English breakfast: une crodie di panzete, un ûf strapassât e une scliçade di fasui tal sugo di pomodoro cuntune tace di lat. O podarès tirâ indelunc cun chest mangjâ par dute la setemane. Doi pascj a cinc sterlinis par cinc dîs al fâs cincuante in totâl. No mâl, ancje se dopo a varessin di fâmi un clisteri o la lavande gastriche. Mi impensi di mê none che e faseve sù la polente cul pugn, e e tocjave, e tocjave ta la morcje. Mangjâ e murî. No jere mai passude, mieze bree di polente dome par se, fam par vieri, miserie nere, a raspâ ta la cite. A la fieste dai anzians e zirave dute contente cu lis fetis di mortadele che i jessivin da la sachete da la gjache. A puedin stâ ben, a la fam no si comande, no si sa par un doman, par cene. Volìnsi ben al è scrit sul furgon da la Caritas. Vierzìn la puarte da la caritât a Sant Pieri, e sierìn la puarte da la misericordie. In vuaite da lis corints a vierzi tantis puartis! Viodarês, viodarês, e à di tornâ la miserie! O sês usâts masse ben a straçâ come massepassûts. Tignî cont, meti vie, sparagnâ, no si pues savê pal avignî, il cjan al tire simpri fûr il vues di sot tiere, al è amì dal om.

Horatio mi cjale intant che al tocje il sugut dai fasoi cul pan.

'Mi domandi se i plâs la gulizion,' mi dîs.

Sigûr, di lecâsi lis mostacjis. Ogni paîs cu la sô culture culinarie. Âstu di meti il spek di Sauris, la fertaie cui ûfs di cjase e i urtiçons, e ce àno in comun i fasoi cjargnei cui Heinz Beans in scjatule? Nuie.

Si vicine la parone, un fregul plui spontanie, cuant che o sin dongje a paiâ. No je une brute femine, un tic British, un pêl impicotide su doi pecoi di gjambis.

'Us aie plasût la gulizion?' nus domande.

Ancjemò!? I ai metût cuindis agns a usâmi al zuf. Cjalt di scotâsi la lenghe cul lat frêt la prime dì, dopo tal indoman, passantdoman e v.i. cul lat bulint a formâ une sorte di budin, un zuf apont. Altri che il bifidus actiregularis pe panze, cu lis bielis fantatis da la publicitât che lizeris a svoletin come paveis!

Horatio al è propit content. Proteinis a buinore. Ogni

domenie un bon brût cu la gjaline plui vecje dal pulinâr. Lusignis di gras che a zirin come barcjis tal plat, dopo vê trotât par oris ta la cite intant di Messe Grande, e di daûr lis talpis di raspâ, il miôr mangjâ. E je dure a cori daûr di un balon, tierce categorie, dal dut scanât e cu la panze che e bruntule. 'Ce fasêso là daûr in difese!?' Une strache che no mi lasse cori tal pantan, e o ai ancje di sintîlis dal alenadôr intune domenie di ploie da la mê adolessence.
'Parcè lu metie in scuadre chel puar zovin? Nol rive nancje a stâ in pîts!' E dopo a cjase a vaî, parcè che no soi come chei altris, mi mancje alc, e la compagnia semplone che mi da fastidi. 'No saraial mighe fenoli?'
No rivavi propit a cjantâ chê cjançonate ludre, tant sporcje, mi vergognavi. Dopo ogni vitorie, al partive l'alenadôr cun vôs di bas. 'E la frice cence pêl, e la frice cence pêl somee une plaie. E l'uciel discjapielât, e l'uciel discjapielât sassin di strade.' E dopo ducj daûr. Une, dôs voltis e vie indenant. 'E met di bevi a chel puar zovin che si bagni la pivide!'
L'orloi dal cjampanili di Heaven Church li ator al bat lis vot. E je ore di sistemâ il cont. Par cortesie al sarès gno dovê di paiâ, distès cuant che si è a curt di bêçs, tirâ fûr il tacuin e je une grande soference. Dividi a la romane e sarès la soluzion miôr, ancje parcè che o vin spindût sù par jù la stesse cifre, ma Horatio si è ufrît di fâmi di vuide, e dispès la amicizie si rinfuarcìs cuntun at di gjenerositât. Ndemo avanti Guglielmo, fati coragjo, che el sol magna e ore!
Un moment di distrazion fatâl. Horatio al sta tabaiant cu la parone. Si viôt che a son in confidence e, come che al capite in circonstancis similis, a fasin colâ il discors su la novitât, su chest omenut, su chest forest che o soi jo.
'Al è un talian, culì a Londre in mission …' i conte

Horatio.

'Sì, sì … par afârs impuartants.' Ce i contio cumò a la siore culì?

'Sì, sì, un impuartant incuintri cuntun professôr che al à insegnât in Italie par tancj agns.'

E stant che mi à metût ta la categorie da lis personis impuartantis, i zonti che o soi di dongje Vignesie.

'Oh sì, Vignesie! La Basiliche di Sant Marc, il Palaç Ducâl, il Puint dai Suspîrs, la gondule! … soi stade là trê voltis. Ce fortunât!'

No propit Vignesie, cuasi une ore e mieze di machine e dôs par cjatâ di parcâ la machine, trê oris sul acelerât che al ferme ogni pissade di cjan.

Horatio al sarà lât in bagn. No lu viôt. No mi lassarà mighe di bessôl cu la parone e il romanç da la sô vite, dal scambi dal anel di impromission cul so morôs in gondule sul Canâl Grant, e il barlumâ da la lune su la aghe darintade, intune cjalde gnot avostane. Man sul tacuin, o sin furlans, o vin patide miserie e spindi al è simpri stât un cantin che al è miôr no tocjâ. Cun grande soference, viodìn di tirâ fûr lis sterlinis che il Comitât pal Amlêt Furlan mi à dât cun grande gjenerositât.

Colp di sene.

'Dut a puest. Al à paiât Horatio,' mi dîs la parone cuntun ridi soradin.

Un sintiment ingredeât mi cjape di plante fûr, un miscliç di sensazions, dividût tra no jessi stât bon di rinfuarcî la amicizie cun Horatio cuntun nobil at di gjenerositât, e une istintive, viliache, ma ancje plasevule sensazion par no vê intacât il piçul capitâl, puartât daûr dal Friûl.

Al jere avonde scontât che mi tocjàs di paiâ, stant che Horatio si è ufrît di acompagnâmi a destinazion. O provi simpri une sensazion di rabie viers me stes, di fastidi, cuant che lis robis no mi van come che o volarès, come che lis vevi pensadis, e o soi simpri pront a incazâmi par l'enesim esempli di indecision.

Velu, ch'al torne dal bagn. Mai trascurâ i detais te vite.

'Horatio, gracie pe gulizion,' i dîs, e dopo o pant il gno malcontent di façade.

'Nol veve … tocjave a mi di paiâ!'

Ignobile tiritere. Tocjave a mi, tocjave a ti. Mi fâs di vuide, mi paie ancje la gulizion e no pues nancje ricambiâ culì sul moment, parcè che un altri ûf cu la panzete brustulide mi mandarès knock out. Une cjicare di aghe bulint cuntun gust indefinît di cafè e podarès jessi la soluzion par ripaiâlu subit.

'No, va ben cussì. A la prossime ocasion!' mi rispuint Horatio cence ombre di dubi.

Cuissà ce che mi tocje di paiâ la prossime volte. O varai di fâ un pocje di economie sul mangjâ se o ai voie di rivâ insom da la setemane. No mi va di sgarfâ tai bidons des scovacis. Une tace di lat te dan cuasi gratis. E pues bastâ a matine, e prime di lâ a durmî par cjapâ sium.

O saludìn la parone che cumò e je in confidence, cun Vignesie che i à viert il cûr intune epifanie di suns, colôrs e profums. Spiritualmentri nô talians o sin plui usâts al biel, a la art da lis nestris citâts, a la maravee dal nestri paisaç, e no presein avonde il lôr valôr se no son i forescj a ricuardânusal. Vignesie e à dismolât un tininin il British aplomb da la siore.

L'INCUINTRI CUN AMLÊT

L'orloi dal cjampanili da la Glesie di St Matthew al bat lis nûf, un sun çondar tal ultin glon des nûf. In compagnie di Horatio si incjaminìn cun pas sigûr dilunc Queensway. Si cjatìn dentri une fole, un moviment di int che e scomedone par cirî di passâ in direzion dal centri, da la fermade da la metrò plui dongje, da la fermade dal autobus. Une procession di int: impleâts vistûts di gale, feminis che a strenzin la borsete menant il cûl tai leggins aderents, piçui flums che des viutis laterâls si butin su la Queensway, di corse, di presse, gjambis che si movin sveltis, sveltis, sveltis intune ignobile premure, par pôre di rivâ tart. Une fulugne di int 'ch'i' non averei creduto che morte tanta n'avesse disfatta.' Dulà larano mai cussì di buride, a pas svelt, tic-e-tac, viers il comun destin?
O buti il voli suntune persone ferme tal mieç da la fole. E cjale fis denant di se, ma no si sa ce che e sta voglant e parcè. La int lu passe sburide di une bande e di chê altre, un flum in plene, lui fer come un cocâl, nissune reazion, nissun fastidi, nol à ben clâr dulà lâ e ce fâ, un fradi. No mi somee une muse gnove, pluitost un paisan, un furlan tal forest, ancje se al è pôc probabil di intivâsi in cognossincis culì a Londre, tra int anonime. Ancje lui mi olme par un moment, nancje il timp di controlâ, di lâ un fregul plui dongje, di provâ a induvinâ. Un atôr, un politic, un zuiadôr o un mone cualsisei come me? Li impalât a viodi il mont che i zire intor. Horatio al tire indelunc cul so pas decîs. Al è dificil stâi daûr. Distès, o ai come la sensazion di jessi inseguît, di vê cualchidun che nus sta daûr. Cui ise mai chê tierce persone che e cjamine simpri dongje di nô? Isal un spirt che nus tormente, une

ossession, un dubi, o un agnul bon che nus segne la strade?

Mi ziri di colp e mal viôt daûr. Un zovin secandul, sporc, cun barbe e cjavei luncs, une cjamese e jeans malsestâts, stranît, un puar biât.

'Amlêt! Sêstu tu?' Lu fermi intun ingorc di int che mi sburte di daûr.

'Amlêt! Contimi di te!' Mi cjale, ma no mi viôt. Al cîr di capî dulà che al è, di capî la situazion pericolose che si cjate denant. Une espression di pôre, di conturbie, di solitudin in chest mondat plen di int che e judiche, e scuarte, e cope. Il mont al à alçade la scorie; dulà colaraie? Une muse blancje, smamide, stufadice, dut sgjavelât, usât a mangjâ ce che al cjate par strade, a durmî li che i capite. Amlêt!

Trops dîs sono che nol sint plui il so non, che nol condivîf afiets, esperiencis cun cualchidun? Al cîr di capî ce che i tocje. Isal pussibil cjatâ par câs un dal to païs a Londre, un dai pôcs che al varès vût gust di viodi, di incuintrâ, di tabaiâ, di sintî dongje? Al olme Horatio, come se alc di strani e invisibil ai cussì clamâts normâi si fos dut concentrât su di lui, il mâl dal mont, un mont che al bruse e al consume. Lui di bessôl, Amlêt, un ostacul, un berdei, un intrîc, miôr sparî par simpri. Un come lui nol pues stâ ca jù, in chest mondat. Nissun mai al podarà capîlu, dâi une man, judâlu a tornâ in ca di chel mont paralêl, il mont dai poetis, dai profetis, dai mats.

'Guildenstern! Rosencrantz!' Amlêt nus berghele di colp, cu la int che si zire a cjalâlu.

'Voaltris doi mi stais cirint, no mo? Lait vie di me, no vuei viodius!'

'No! O soi jo, Guglielmo di Cjamìn. No mi cognossistu?'

'Vie, vie! No stait a vicinâsi! No stait a tocjâmi!' il puaret al busine inmò plui fuart, cu lis mans denant di se a protezion.

'Disimi che tu sês tu, Amlêt, che no mi confont, che une strane cumbinazion nus à fat cjatâ culì a Londre. Isal mai pussibil?' O cîr di confuartâlu su lis mês reâls intenzions.

'No soi l'Amlêt che tu ciris, l'Amlêt che al passe par mat, il basoâl che ducj a coionin, il mone che si paie di bevi par ridii daûr ...'

'Oh, tu sês propit tu, il gno paisan!'

'No cate che la int no mi crodi, o soi l'ultin erêt da la nobile famee dai marchês da Cjamìn,' al pant Amlêt un tininin cuietât.

'Va ben, no mi impuarte se tu sês l'Amlêt che o cognòs, o, come che tu mi contis, l'Amlêt da la nobile famee dai marchês da Cjamìn. Il fat impuartant al è che si sin cjatâts culì a Londre, in mieç di une conturbie di int, robe impussibile. Di no crodi! Nô doi che o vignìn di un piçul paîs, di une piçule patrie. Al devi jessi propit un segn dal destin. Al veve di sucedi e vonde, une fatalitât.'

'No sta vignîmi dongje! No sta vualmâmi cussì!' al vose Amlêt intune sorte di deliri.

Lu sai ce che al pense di me, dut sporc come ch'o soi, cu la barbe e i cjavei luncs. Un diviers, un che nol è stât bon di fâ nuie inte vite. O sai che no mi lavi, che o fâs stomi. Un mat che nol à un puest dulà stâ in chest mont, nol pues vê une famee che i sta dongje e lu jude. No ai mai volût vê a cefâ cun lôr, cu la parintât, cui paisans. Cun gno pari si sin simpri cridâts. No tu sês bon di nuie. Jo a la tô etât o savevi ce fâ inte vite. Ma jo no jeri come lui, no soi mai stât e no vuei jessi come lui. Lu sai, lu viôt che mi spiete un futûr diferent. Al è par cheste reson che o soi vignût a cirîlu culì a Londre. E dopo o larai bintar in zîr pal mont. Ducj nô o vin dirit a un futûr diferent. Gno pari mi à simpri umiliât. No tu rivis, o scugnìn jessi pazients cun te, une vore pazients. Ce vâstu mai a scuele? No je fate par te. Se tu cjatis un lavorut, sot paron a imparâ un mistîr, la bustute a la fin dal mês... No si pues pratindi cuntun come te. Lu ai viodût ch'al pendolave come un salam di une trâf da la tieze. No vevi inmò cutuardis agns, e soi lât subite a clamâ gno nono che strissinantsi sù par la scjale al è vignût a viodi, e dopo si e poiât jù, di no stâ impins, lis mans su la muse. Si è metût a vaî. Nol voleve che lu cjalàs, e jo cul cûr che mi sclopave, e mi sintivi rivoltâ il stomi di gjavâmi il respîr. E no olsavi a cjalâ di chê bande, chê robe che e pendolave, di viodile simpri di gnot prime di cjapâ sium, di colp jù pal dì, une ossession, un torment di no podê dismenteâ. 'Une vergogne, une vergogne!' al continuave a ripeti il nono e nol voleve clamâ nissun. 'Ce puedie pensâ la int? Une vergogne!!' al continuave a ripeti al infinît. O soi tornât jù da la scjale par lâ a vaî daûr la cjase, su la roste. Mi à viodût un om che al lavorave tal cjamp li dongje. 'Ce âstu frut? Parcè vaistu?' Al è di in chê volte che o ai començât a vê alucinazions. Mi plaseve stâ di bessôl, no viodi nissun, dome jo e gno nono. Par vinci la solitudin, o levi sul cjast o su la tieze cun intor une sorte di gaban par deventâ un dai miei erois, un mît invincibil. Mat, mi disevin i paisans cuant che o ziravi di bessôl dilunc la roste di sore sere, e o scjampavi di lôr. Un salvadi che nol pues vê ben ta la vite. Ma jo mi soi simpri freât da la int, e o ai let, studiât, fin a cjatâ fûr cui che o soi veramentri. Ognidun di nô al è dentri di se cualchidun altri che nol rive a saltâ fûr.

'Amlêt, alore tu mi cognossis! Tu sâs cui che o soi. Lasse che ti disi trop content che o soi di vioditi.' O voi plui dongje par imbraçâlu, ma Amlêt mi ten a distance cuntune man.

'Cui ti mandie a cirîmi culì a Londre? Guildenstern, la tô cjalade ti tradìs!'

'Nin mo Amlêt! Dome il câs nus à fat cjatâ culì a Londre. No mi mande nissun!'

'Rosencrantz, chel om cun te, ti à mandât a cirîmi!'

'No, Amlêt! Al è un londinês, une brave persone che o ai cognossût vuê a buinore suntune bancjine di Hyde Park. Si è ufiert di acompagnâmi di un ciert professôr Brough. Spiete chi un moment che lu informi su di te.'

O voi viers Horatio che si è fermât a spietânus cualchi pas plui indenant.

'Horatio, no lu fâs spietâ, nomo? Mi soi intivât cun chest compagn dal gno stes paîs. No isal incredibil?'

'Ben. O podìn cjoli un cafè cun lui.' Horatio al sugjerìs un locâl li dongje che al cognòs ben.

'No i va trop la compagnie. No pensi che al vedi intenzion di fermâsi cun nô,' i dîs.

Horatio al intuìs la situazion un tininin ingredeade e al cjate une scuse par dânus la pussibilitât di sclarîsi.

'No stait a fâsi problemis. Us spieti. Va ben?'

'Gracie, Horatio.'

'O doi un cuc a chel negozi là jù, e o torni tra cualchi minût.'

Al travierse la strade par jentrâ intun negozi di anticuariât.

Jo e Amlêt si tirìn un pôc in bande dal passaç par capî miôr la incredibile circostance che nus à fat cjatâ in centri a Londre.

'Amlêt, disimi alc di te. Ce fâstu culì a Londre? Lavoristu?'

'Simpri cun domandis! Ducj compagns. Dulà vâstu, ce fâstu, ducj cuancj a rutin fûr!'

'O volevi dome comunicâti la mê sorprese, il plasê di vioditi intun moment che no mi spietavi ...'

'L'om no mi plâs,' Amlêt mi dîs di colp tirant fûr ricuarts des sôs leturis.

'O viôt che lis lezions che ti ai dât su Shakespeare ti àn zovât. Tu saressis pront par une recite,' i dîs cuntun fregul di ironie.

'Nissune recite! E je la storie da la mê vite, la stesse storie dal princip Amlêt.'

'Scuse, o scherçavi,' i dîs cirint di no ufindilu.

'O soi il vêr Amlêt, dome jo, l'ultin fi da la gjernazie maledete dai da Cjamìn. Ve chi l'anel d'arint che o ten simpri cun me, blason dai marchês da Cjamìn.'

'Jo ti crôt, ma distès al somee dut strani. Chest nestri incuintri al jere predestinât. Il destin nus à fat cjatâ. Amlêt, tu jentris ancje tu ta la mê visite a Londre.'

'Come che o ai nasât subit. Ti àn mandât a cirîmi par sierâmi intun manicomi!'

'No, spiete che ti conti …'

'Dome cualchi mês, ti prometin. Pal to ben … Tu cjolis chestis cidelis pal gnervôs e tu starâs subit miôr. E dopo altris cidelis, simpri miôr di chês che tu cjolevis prime, fin cuant che no tu sâs dulà che tu sês e ce che a fasin di te. Ti trimin lis mans … O vin intenzion di fâti alc tal cerviel …'

'Nuie di dut chest. Ti zuri, Amlêt. Ti zuri! Sta a sintîmi che ti conti la novitât. La tô convinzion, che ti à puartât fin culì a Londre, e je che tu sês un nobil, l'ultin erêt da la famee estinte dai da Cjamìn di Trevîs, nomo?'

'Lu sint dentri di me. Une vôs mal dîs di continui. Tu âs di vinci la pôre da la pôre, la pôre dal dubi, da la difidence da la int comune che ti invelene il sanc. Tu tu apartegnis a la int elete. Tu sês clamât par fâ grandis robis, nassût cu la cjamese. Cjape sù la plante di fenoli e bat la ziringè …'

'Lasse pierdi chestis robis cumò. O stavi par dîti che ancje Shakespeare al somee che al fos a cognossince dai

marchês da Cjamìn, almancul seont il parê di un medievalist di fame, un ciert professôr Brough.'
Amlêt par nuie maraveât al somee cumò vignîmi daûr, e vê pal moment dismenteât il suspiet, la pôre, di finî internât intun manicomi.
'Shakespeare al è simpri stât la mê ossession,' mi dîs. 'Mal insumii di gnot. O ai imparât dute la tragjedie *Amlêt* a memorie par cirî un contat cun lui. O scuen lâ a Stratford-upon-Avon su la sô tombe par sintî la vicinance, par comunicâ cun lui. O ai tantis robis di domandâi ...'
'Un dì o podìn lâ insiemi,' i dîs par vinci la sô difidence.
'Va ben, ma cumò o ai di lâ. No vuei che il siôr là vie mi puarti dentri inta la sô cliniche psichiatriche. Mi cirin pardut, ma no mi cjataran tant facil.'
'Cui? Horatio? Al è un insegnant di inglês in pension. Cuant che al torne, o nin drets di chest professôr Brough che, come che o stavi par dîti, al crôt, al è convint che Shakespeare si fos ispirât ai nobii da Cjamìn par scrivi la tragjedie *Amlêt*.'
'*Amlêt* di Shakespeare?' mi domande straneât, simpri plui cjapât dentri da la storie. 'Si faseve passâ par mat par scuvierzi la veretât su la muart dal pari,' mi dîs. 'Jo invezit par dismenteâ la muart di gno pari.'
'No volevi dîtal, ma tu mi someis plui a puest di tancj sogjets che a zirin libars. La tô mi somee dute une recite e la malatie une sielte studiade. O viôt tantis coincidencis che a fasin deventâ cheste facende plui che une ricercje storiche une sorte di cjace a fantasimis di un passât lontan. Secont il parê di chest professôr, la tragjedie *Amlêt* di Shakespeare e sarès leade a la storie dai tiei antenâts, e di precîs a Riçart Secont da Cjamìn, probabilmentri copât di so fradi Guecelon il cinc di Avrîl dal mil tresinte e dodis.'
'O scuen cirî un contat cun Shakespeare e viodi di capî lis

robis che lui al saveve, e che jo no soi inmò rivât a capî sul gno passât. O ai di lâ a Stratford su la sô tombe. O sint di jessi dongje da la veretât.'

'Po stâi, ma prin ti consei di vignî cun nô dal professôr Brough che, di sigûr, al devi vê scuviert alc altri sul câs dal Amlêt furlan.'

Cumò il fantat mi ven daûr cun atenzion e mi scjampe di jessi un fregul ironic, forsi pe strache e la plombe che mi cres dentri.

'Cuissà ce content che al sarès il president dal Comitât pal Amlêt Furlan, se al scuvierzès che Amlêt, nevôt dal vecjo mulinâr, nol è un mat, fûr di cjâf, ma l'anel che al pues colegâ Shakespeare cui marchês di Trevîs. Cjamìn al Tiliment al podarès zimulâsi cu la citât danese di Helsingør, dulà che la tragjedie e je ambientade, e deventâ un centri mondiâl di studis Shakespearians.'

Dopo un pôc viodint il zovin pluitost pinsirôs a rivuart di events cussì inspietâts, o zonti cuntun ridi soradin:

'Amlêt, ti puartaressin in procession cu la bande!'

'Us cognòs ben jo, ducj voaltris! O vês voie di puartâmi dentri cu lis vuestris stupidis mignassis!' Amlêt al pant une vore urtât.

'Scuse tant. Mi sint scunît. Dut ce che al sta sucedint mi somee cussì assurt che mi à fat pierdi il cjâf.'

Guglielmo al è une brave persone. Mi à simpri volût ben. Cumò mi invide a lâ di chest professôr cun lui e Rosencrantz, che no mi somee un dai stricecerviei che mi àn vût in cure in passât. Aio di acetâ? No varès reson, distès dopo tant torzeonâ, tu sintis la dibisugne, il calôr di scambiâ cuatri peraulis cun cualchidun. Un mandi sintût cul cûr, o ancje dome sintî il sunôr da la tô lenghe intun paîs forest, une sensazion che ti cor jù pe schene, ti impie une lûs dentri.

'Va ben. O ven cun te dal professôr, ma cence chel Rosencrantz che mi sta daûr.'

'Horatio? No podìn. Al cognòs la strade e al è une brave persone. Al pues judâ ancje te se propit tu vuelis restâ a Londre, cuant che jo o tornarai in Friûl.'

'Va ben, ma parcè no restistu culì a Londre?' mi domande cun afiet.

'No, o scuen tornâ. No ai i bêçs par stâ culì, e la mê famee mi spiete in Friûl. No soi bintar come te, no mi sint di lâ ator pal mont cence la ciertece di tornâ intun puart sigûr. Il gnûf, il diviers mi metin simpri pôre, la fuarce di gravitât mi atrai viers un mont piçul di afiets e amôr che forsi no ai mai vût fin cumò. E dopo tal ai za dit che o soi culì par cheste mission dal Comitât che salacor e pues puartâ vantaçs a dut il teritori, e ancje a mi se dut si cumbine.'

'Jo no tornarai plui a Cjamìn. Mi fâs fin sens la int! Par lôr o soi il mat di sierâ intun manicomi. Miôr vivi libar, di siums, di ilusions ... Velu Rosencrantz che al torne, pront a puartâmi cun se.'

'Salve Horatio!' i voi incuintri e i spieghi la gnove situazion. 'Il gno paisan culì al à decidût di vignî cun nô dal professôr Brough. Nol è un probleme, nomo?'

'Nancje par insium. Al è benvignût,' mi rispuint cu la ande disponibile che lu caraterize.

Horatio, Hamlet e William. O vin l'autôr, i atôrs e nus mancje il regjist. Il professôr Brough al podarès fâ la regjie da la nestre comedie. O ise une tragjedie? O viodarìn cuant che o sarìn cul professôr. Lu decidarà lui. O sin cuasi rivâts.

LA VISITE A LA FORRESTER COURT CARE HOME

Forrester Court Care Home e je une costruzion su doi plans, stîl Vitorian, intune zone cuiete di Londre, frecuentade di int di passaç viers la stazion dai trens di Paddington o i uficis da la aministrazion da la capitâl. No je une zone residenziâl e nancje turistiche. Un puartelut cun trê scjalins e un curt passaç contornâts di rosis nus puarte al ingrès.

Une infermiere nus ven incuintri.

'Bundì. Puedio jessi di aiût?'

'Bundì. O volaressin tabaiâ cul professôr Brough,' i spieghi il motîf da la nestre visite.

'Che al scusi. Vêso dit professôr...?'

'Professôr Brough. B.R.O.U.G.H,' i dîs franc lis letaris dal cognon.

'No vin nissun professôr culì che jo o savedi,' nus dîs.

'O soi sigûr che al è chi. Puedie controlâ sul computer?' i domandi cun cortesie.

'Forsi nol è chi di tant timp. O voi a controlâ.'

'Gracie.'

Cumò al ven fûr che il professôr Brough nol è chi, o piês ancjemò che chest professôr nol esist, nol è mai esistût, o come che al sucêt intes comediis di Shakespeare, al è dome un scambi di identitât o un insium. 'E chest motîf flap e barbôs nol à plui consistence di un sium,' si pues lei in Shakespeare.

Vele che e torne la infermiere cuntun riduçâ divertît e pôc confuartant, ch'al pant plui di tantis peraulis.

'Che mi scusi tant! Sì, il siôr Brough. O sin cussì usâts a clamâlu il poete, che o vin cuasi dismenteât il so vêr non. Al è simpri che al continue a 'sabaiâ di bessôl cun cualchidun che si clame a pressapôc Sheikh Spear. Al sarà un arap, o pensi.'

Ve chi, un dai plui grancj esperts di Shakespeare al trabascje cuntun arap. E je za començade la demolizion dal personaç. Il professôr Brough che al çavarie di bessôl cuntun seic di Dubai. Dulà ise finide dute la sô storie passade tes universitâts, il rispietôs silenzi, la devozionâl atenzion tes cunvignis di mieze Europe? Vanitas, vanitatum. Sflocjâ e smenâsi une ore in sene prime dal grant cidinôr. Mîts che si frucin, categoriis che si anulin tal inesorabil avanzâ dal timp. Il rispiet cuasi devozionâl viers l'autoritât une robe di altris timps. Mi impensi dal predi in paîs, une figure impuartante, al veve il rispiet di ducj. 'Sia lodato Gesù Cristo.' Di picinin, i ai dit al gnûf plevan. Mi à cjalât cun maravee, come par dî: 'Dulà soio mai capitât?' Mi à spedît cuntun mandi, e jo frut, dut scaturît, li a spietâ il 'Sempre sia Lodato' che nol è mai rivât di in chê volte. Crodincis che a van a fâsi benedî, la fede che si sfante, ducj compagns, o cirìn di dâ un sens a la nestre vite prime di sparî par simpri. Mi ven di pensâ ai grancj personaçs, grancj insegnants, che o ai cognossût tes scuelis di mieç Friûl, tes mês suplencis. Si devin une impuartance grandonone cuant che a cjapavin la peraule tes riunions. Cumò, nissun al sa nuie di lôr. Prof. Cjossul al vâl come il doi di briscule, la sô batule e je stade une meteore, e nancje i mûrs da la Aule Magne a àn plui un ricuart di lui. No mi impensi plui dai lôr nons. Sprofondâts tal abìs. Plui nuie. Parcè vino di creâsi tantis ilusions di grandece, se dopo ducj nô o finìn in dismentie? Lis peraulis dai oms a son limitadis parcè che al è limitât lui, tal so timp e tal so spazi. Nuie si salve al falçut dal timp che al sesele il racolt.

'Podêso spietâ il professôr ta la sale?' nus dîs la

infermiere.

'Lu puartarai là se al è sveât ta la sô cjamare.'

'Sì, sigûr.'

'Par plasê, us racomandi di tabaiâi a planc e clâr, di no alçâ il ton da la vôs o inrabiâsi,' nus zonte cun ande professionâl. 'O savês, al patìs di demezie senîl.'

'Va ben. Gracie.'

La infermiere e jes svelte dal ingrès e e sparìs dilunc il coridôr viers lis cjamaris.

'Crist ve dûl di nô!' mi ven di pensâ li sul moment.

Si sentìn suntun vecjo sofà da la sale in spiete dal professôr. Cui braçs in crôs o pesìn il pro e il cuintri. La struture modeste che lu ospite, la infermiere ignorante che i sta daûr, e cemût che lu à presentât, il poete che al tabaie di bessôl cuntun ciert Sheikh Spear, mi ven di pensâ che il professôr Brough al sedi un puar vecjo malât, di passe otante agns, cu la ment malsestade.

I voi fis sul tocut di cîl blu fûr dal barcon, come in ospedâl a ritirâ lis analisis, cui numars che a corin lents, a un pas dal judizi finâl, e la voie di jessi fûr in mont, dulà che il cîl al somee di tocjâlu. In chei moments là sù in Cjargne, tu rivis fin a pensâ che il mont nol sedi dome caos, ma al esisti un progjet, un dissen precîs, e la perfezion dal creât no sedi dome une leç fisiche, ma la creazion di une ment superiôr, e par un moment tu pensis di volê ben a ducj, di perdonâ i nemîs, di començâ une altre vite e di jessi eterni. Signôr ve dûl di nô.

Horatio al somee divertît, e al vîf la situazion cun spiete, cul spirt pragmatic dai inglês, là che jo invezit o vîf l'incuintri cun ansie e la pôre dal sigûr faliment.

Amlêt, pierdût tal so mont, al pâr cjapât in fantasiis maladis. Une sfese di lûs dal barcon che e ilumine un mont discognossût, un rumôr, une fuarte dissonance, lis mans su lis orelis par fermâ chê violence, l'urli di Munch, scossis di energjie tun cerviel malât. Vivi intun mont paralêl, intune realtât insumiade, il mont dai artiscj, dai visionaris, dai mats, di ducj nô che no vin finît di crodi. O sin fats da la stesse sostance dai insiums; e la nestre vite cussì curte e je contornade di sium.

Si sintin dai pas strissinâts sul paviment, e un murmuiâ continui.

'No, no, no! Lassimi di bessôl! ... No soio bon di cjaminâ?! Vie! No ai voie di viodi nissun!' il professôr Brough al pant il so malcontent.

'No sta vê fastidi, poete! A son amîs. A àn voie di fevelâ cun te,' la infermiere e cîr di cuietâlu.

'Oh, no sta clamâmi poete! Vie di cheste marmaie mate. Vie, vie di chest mont malât!' al berle.

Il professôr Brough al ven indenant a scats, tignintsi sù cuntune mace, controlât da la infermiere. Al è un omenut ingobît, sui otante, cjavei grîs e sbarlufîts, spilocs di barbe i cressin ca e là suntune muse grispose. La cjaladure fisse e pant che nol viôt ben, e nol ricognòs lis personis che al à denant di se. La infermiere e cîr di acompagnâlu, ma il professôr, une vore urtât, le poche vie cuntune man.

'O provi disgust a cjalâti!' i busine cuintri.

'Sta bon, vecjut!'

Si pues ben capî che il professôr Brough al è stât obleât a vignî chi, cuintri la sô volontât. Situazions similis si ripetin dispès, dulà che lui i ten a la sô autonomie, ancje se al viôt che il cuarp nol ubidìs plui ai comants dal cerviel, e il cerviel nol da il just jutori. Il puar om si inacuarç di no jessi plui lui, di no vê il control di ce che al sta fasint, e al viôt il mont reâl sfantâsi cun dutis lis personis che lu contornin. Dut si confont, l'impussibilitât di gjestî il presint e blecs di passât, framents di ricuarts che a vegnin fûr bot e sclop come lusignis che si impiin e a muerin. Dople rabiade, cuintri chei che lu judin e cuintri se stes, cuintri il mont e il destin malandret di deventâ vecjos e murî.

La infermiere lu acompagne a sentâsi denant di nô. Operazion un grum laboriose, fate di moviments denant e indaûr, fin a zirucâ cuntune colade a plomp su la poltrone.

'Bundì, professôr Brough,' lu saludi cun gracie.

'Bundì,' al murmuie cuntun fâ rassegnât, pôc usât a la compagnie. Ma al è dome un moment, parcè che l'estri si fâs plui disponibil, fin curiôs.

'O pensi di cognossilu, e di cognossi lis altris dôs personis. Distès, o soi inciert, parcè che pal plui o soi ignorant … talians, nomo?'

'Sì, nô doi o sin talians.'

'Cemût si clamial lui?'

'Mi clami Guglielmo, e i miei doi amîs a son Horatio e Amlêt.'

'Il so non al è William par inglês, nomo? Come William Shakespeare! Il poete. Isal lui stât culì îr?'

'Oh no. No jeri jo. Îr a cheste ore mi cjatavi inmò in Friûl.'

'Mi àn dite che cualchidun al sarès rivât vuê o doman … mi àn dite talians … Cui lu à dit? Mi àn puartât vie dutis lis mês robis. No ai plui une pene par scrivi, par segnâ i miei pinsîrs, lis mês ideis, par podê ricuardâju! La mê memorie e va simpri piês … di zornade in zornade … no viôt che la mê memorie e ledi in miôr. No plui.'

'Che no lu disi, professôr Brough! Cui sa mai ce che il doman al puartarà,' lu confuarte Horatio. 'Mai pierdi la sperance!'

'Doman, e doman, e doman, di zornade in zornade … Al cognòs William Shakespeare, il poete, nomo?'

'Sì, oh sì … Macbeth, cuint at, sene cuinte!' Horatio al mostre interès, ma jo o comenci a pierdi la sperance pal tabaiâ assurt dal professôr.

'Siôr Brough, Shakespeare al va benon, ma o volarès che lui mi disès alc sul *Amlêt.*' O provi a esplorâ ce ricuarts che il professôr al à da la tragjedie *Amlêt.*

'O sês amants di Shakespeare! ... O sês poetis! … Lui us à mandâts culì!' al pense che o sin in mission par cont dal grant poete inglês.

'Oh no, professôr Brough. No nus mande Shakespeare,' i rispuint pluitost rassegnât.

'O soi chi cun chescj miei amîs in mission a rivuart da lis fonts dal *Amlêt* ...' o cîr di spiegâi il vêr motîf da la nestre visite, ma o ven subit intorot.

'Amîs, amîs … ducj nô o vin bisugne di volê ben a cualchidun su la vie viers il paîs inesplorât …' al cite il professôr.

'... Di dulà che no torne anime vive,' o completi la citazion dal *Amlêt* di Shakespeare pensant plui al impussibil tornâ di ca da la ment umane disturbade che al tornâ di ca dopo la muart, dal famôs monolic, *'Jessi o no jessi'.*

'Al à citât Shakespeare! Ancje lui al è un poete … che mi fâsi pensâ ... L'amì insegnant che o vevi a Vicenze al jere come lui, la stesse espression lambicade tai voi … Une volte i ai domandât se al stave ben, se al jere content. Mi à dit che al veve la femine, i fîs e une biele cjase … che mi à maraveât. Al scuen vê vût alc … cun chê espression stranide che al veve … Al capite cuant che mancul tu tal spietis. Tra i cuarante e i cincuante. Etât critiche … si comence a inacuarzisi dai nestris faliments … O ai insegnât ta la Universitât di Vicenze. Cognossial Vicenze?'

'O sin di Udin, dongje Vicenze.'

'Puedial dîmi cemût che si scrîf?'

'U-D-I-N-E,' i silabi lis letaris come che al è in ûs in Ingletiere.

'Sì, o cognòs il puest, ma no mi impensi dulà che lu ai sintût. La mê memorie no je ben ... us prei, no stait menâmi ator. O soi un puar ninin di vecjo incocalît ... no sai dulà che o soi cumò. Soio intun bordel? E ce fâsio culì? Ancje se voaltris mi disês cui che o sês e ce che o volês ... doi minûts e dut al sparìs. Dismenteât, cancelât ... Scusait ma il gno cjâf nol funzione tant ben ... Un vecjo al è un odeôs pipinot. Decrepit. La plui schifose misture di puce oribile che e vedi mai ufindût il nâs. Podaraio mai lâ in miôr? O ai pierdude la sperance.'

O cjali cun compassion il puar, vecjo professôr. Tai siei voi un grant dolôr a viodisi in chel stât. Di sigûr al à vût la sô part di glorie te vite. Onôrs che i àn puartât notorietât e fortune, e dut ce che ur ven daûr. Al somee cumò, ma al jere za dut scrit cuant che o sin nassûts che se o vin la fortune di vivi a lunc, clamìnle fortune, o varìn di passâ ducj cuancj par chê condizion alì, umii e prepotents, puars e siôrs. Ciert, al zove se un al à la pussibilitât di restâ tal so ambient, al rive a vê cualchi pont di riferiment cul so passât. Ma chest al è simpri mancul pussibil. Dut câs, un tentatîf o ai di fâlu par viodi se il mît dal *Amlêt* furlan al è une invenzion da la rêt, fake news, come che lis fasin passâ cumò.

'Siôr Brough, di sigûr si ricuarde ce che il professôr Clough, so colaboradôr e amì, al à scuviert su *Romeo and Juliet* a Udin,' i motivi la ricercje dal professôr Clough.

'Ce aial scuviert? No mi impensi cumò,' mi domande cui voi che mi fissin cence espression.

'Il professôr Clough al à scrit che la tragjedie *Romeo and Juliet* no à nuie a cefâ cu la citât di Verone, parcè che i Capulets e i Montagues ...'

'La peste su lis dôs fameis! Sì, sì. La vere storie no je di Verone, ma di une citât li dongje.'
'Udin.'
'Oh sì, Udin … che mi fasi pensâ … dulà isal di precîs? Ce strade di chi? Italy, dîsio ben? Paddington, West End e dopo a drete o a çampe? Oh sì, su la rive sud dal Tamigi, al scuen jessi dongje dal Globe, o pensi …'
Sì, di là da la aghe, Tamigi, Tiliment … al è dut un altri mont, forest e discognossût, come ta la ment di chest puar om, dispierdût tal cidin di un grant passât. La memorie e je come cerclis di lûs che si impiin mo chi mo là, barconetis tal scûr di une ment malade. Un cercli luminôs che nus contorne dal inizi a la fin. Flash di ricuarts, flics di storiis metudis adun: Italie, Ingletiere, Friûl … dut un messedot. Puar vecjo, puars nô.
'Ma cui isal lui, e lis dôs personis culì?' mi domande di gnûf. 'Mal à dit prime, nomo? Oh! Ce che mi tocje cumò, amì plui cjâr, dut ce che o sai al sparìs a la fin. Oh! No cognòs nissun. Cui aial dit Guglielmo? Il Concuistadôr? Nol jere cun me a Hastings, nomo?'
Jo, Guglielmo il concuistadôr? La uniche robe che o soi rivât a concuistâ cun fadie al è stât chel toc di cjarte cun su scrit 'dotôr', pal rest, sedi il lavôr che la famee a son stâts une rese plui che une concuiste. Demenzie senîl. Brute robe. Flics di pinsîrs che si corin daûr, la balute che e zire svelte su la roulette e si ferme suntun numar par formâ gnovis combinazions, une gnove vision dal mont, dulà che spazi e timp no esistin plui, vuê e doman a son compagns, i vîfs e i muarts a son insiemi e si tabain, odi e amôr viers lis personis si cumbinin prime e dopo mangjât, prime di lâ a durmî o dopo sveâts, circuits che si tocjin o si distachin tal cerviel, a impiin une lûs, si vierç une barconete suntune passion zovanîl, ve, di colp, si cumbine cuntun tuart subît

e l'odi viers la persone che lu à perpetrât. E dut al devente
odi: dal stât presint, da la persone che e je li dongje e ti
assist, di dut il mont. Vie, vie, muart di fam, piel di sbilf,
lenghe di vacje scridelide, bigul di toro, bacalà!
Ancje cheste mê mission a Londre e podarès finî culì, ma
parcè no provâ a tirâ fûr alc di positîf ancje dai câs plui
disperâts. Amlêt al riduce e si pues intuî che al sta ben cun
nô. Al à compagnie e il trabascjâ dal professôr lu
incuriosìs, lu poche a cjatâ il fîl dal glimuç ingredeât dai
siei monolics. Magari al è bon di cjatâ un sens al so deliri.
In realtât, Amlêt al è concentrât suntune spere di soreli che
e filtre di daûr la tende, e e finìs la sô corse su la man
grispade dal professôr Brough sul braçâl da la poltrone.
Inta la lûs, e somee la man di pape Nozent X tal cuadri di
Bacon, cu lis venis blu infûr su la piel lisse, rams turchins
dal flum Tiliment tes gravis inceants da la pedemontane
furlane.
Al è strani che dopo tant zirâ a vueit par Londre di bessôl
cirint di procurâ il mangjâ tai cassonets e durmî li che al
capite, mi cjati culì in compagnie di int che mi clame par
non ... Amlêt ... Al è biel sintî il nestri non dopo tant timp.
Int che ti sta a sintî, no ti pare vie, anzit, ti fâs part da la lôr
vite. E chest vecjo culì, jo lu capìs benon, sospendût intun
mont dome so, cence lis regulis e lis mil fufignis che a
lambichin la esistence tal mont malât di vuê. La man
antighe dal professôr sul braçâl da la poltrone, il cuarp di
Matusalem, la sô inteligjence di profete, saràial mai stât a
viodi alc dal mont di là? Cui soio jo? Amlêt, veramentri?
Cuâl isal il gno destin e cuâl saressial stât se o fos nassût
siôr o intune altre famee, intun altri paîs? E se no fos
nassût, cui varessial cjapât il gno puest?
Ducj chei che mi ridin daûr, mi coionin, mi pain di bevi
par viodimi fâ il stupit, come tirâ sù la suste di un pipinot

par viodilu balâ un moment, chê int alì, ce saie di se, ce ch'e sta fasint, dulà che e sta lant, o ise come a *rolling stone* che e rodole jù tal vueit da la lôr esistence? Cemût si sintisi a jessi un nuie pardabon? Jo o soi sigûr che ta la mê chimiche al è scrit un destin diferent. Mi viôt come il princip *Amlêt* che si rint cont di jessi destinât a grandis impresis, ma nol rive a acetâ il mâl dal mont, nol rive a diliberâsi dai dubis che lu tormentin. Al distruç se stes, la sô famee, come i marchês da Cjamìn, i miei vons, che a rivin fin a copâsi tra fradis, e a sparissin da la storie subit dopo. Il destin di ducj i oms che a pierdin il cjâf pal podê. Ce ise cheste cuintessence da la cinise? L'om no mi plâs. Jo no vuei jessi cussì … Mat, mi clamin, ma lôr rivino a viodisi dentri cui che a son, dulà che a stan lant?

UNE FACENDE INTRIGOSE

Un moment di strache, un moment di meditazion, un moment sacri, diliberâsi dal pês dal cuarp e vongolâ intune vite paralele. La identitât dal professôr Brough si sfante intun mont grîs e impalpabil. Cjapât dal disconfuart, o cjali il puar vecjo cui voi che si sierin a pôc a pôc, e un fîl di bave che i ven fûr da la bocje e i cor jù pal smursiel.
Cui sino? Dulà stino lant? Cui isal che al vuarde il nestri cjamin? Il nuie? L'istint da la furmiute che e cor svelte al furmiâr, o un Ent Superiôr, Diu? Il Diu di Abram? Aial la barbe Mister Godot? Bionde o ... blancje?
Podaressial mai il Diu paron, cu la barbe blancje, vecjo carampan, risolvi i nestris dubis? Ti domandi il sacrifici dal to unic fi. Tu âs di copâlu, sacrificâlu a la mê glorie. Ma sino fûr cul cjâf? Abram di passe cent agns al varà vût un tic di Alzaheimer, no ti dîs cumò, ma distès, cemût si fasial a copâ l'unic fi? Ancje se a fossin stâts dîs, dodis: Primo, Secondo ... Firmino.
Ce Diu dal balon che al zire lis robis cemût che i pâr! Al sta da la tô bande. Paradîs sigurât se tu copis l'infedêl. Al è come te, compagn di te, ma al è nassût tal paîs dongje, stes soreli, stessis gjondis e patiments, ma i àn insegnât une altre lenghe, une altre culture, une altre religjon. No varìno mighe di copâlu par chest? E in percentuâl, ce pussibiltâts vino di indreçâ il nestri destin seont i nestris desideris? Isal tant miôr jessi simpri al centri da lis robis, e po dopo sintî plui fuart il vueit, il frêt da la esistence, cuant che chei altris ti abandonin e tu deventis vecjo e dirocât?
Mister Brough al vierç i voi dopo il lizêr inçussiment. L'efiet da lis midisinis che lu calmin, lu indurmidissin, ma i fasin pierdi la cussience dal mont reâl, a cancelin chel

sbrendul di memorie che al met adun lis relazions tra lis personis.

Mi cjale fis cuntun ridi soradin, content di jessi ancjemò tra i vîfs.

'Cui isal lui? Ancjemò chi?' mi torne a domandâ.

'O soi Guglielmo. Lui no mi cognòs, ma jo sì che lu cognòs! Professôr te Universitât di Vicenze. Critic di Shakespeare e espert da la Rinassince inglese ...'

'Sì, sì, ma jo o cîr di capî parcè che lui mi cognòs ... Jo o ami la Italie, ma al è un an che no torni plui a Vicenze ... o sono passâts dîs agns? ... No mi impensi. Pûr, o soi inciert cumò, sierât in cheste cjase. O ignori dal dut ce puest che al è chest culì, e il gno talent. No viôt nissun. Mi sint di bessôl, tant di bessôl ... la zoventût e je passade di un grum di agns. Cuant che o jeri rampit tal judizi, cul sanc frêt, par fâ come che o fasevi une volte ... Ce aio fat vuê? Nuie. Ce aio fat îr? No mi impensi ... Al è un mont di ombris, cîi oribii ... Oh mi ven voie di vaî!' il professôr al finìs il sbroc cuntun lament di dûl viers se stes.

'Mister Brough, in Italie si crôt che la vere storie di *Amlêt* e sedi sucedude te Marcje trevisane e no in Danimarche,' i dîs, pôc convint di rivâ a impiâ une lûs inta la ment scunide dal professôr.

'Peraulis, peraulis, peraulis ... Fevele plui clâr, fantat!' Mi soi dismenteât da la racomandazion da la infermiere di tabaiâi a planc e clâr.

'Professôr, in Italie a pensin che la tragjedie *Amlêt* no sedi sucedude tal cjistiel di Elsinore in Danimarche ...'

'Lui al à dit Elsinore, al à dit dal *Princip Amlêt ... la tiere no mi somee altri che une schifose e pucelente congregazion di vapôrs,'* il professôr mi interomp par fâmi capî cu la citazion dal *Amlêt* il so pinsîr su la gjernazie umane.

Al à induvinât la mê convinzion cence savê il vêr motîf da la mê visite culì a Londre. Lui nus conte di une pucelente congregazion di vapôrs, jo di cacan. Simpri alc che al smorbee. A voltis, ciertis alchimiis a vegnin fûr par câs, par sinestesie, e nus dan il sens di dulà che o sin e di dulà che o stin lant. Distès, la reson o ai di cjatâle dal parcè che in Friûl a pensin che la font dal *Amlêt* di Shakespeare e sedi in cualchi mût leade a Riçart e Guecelon, marchês di Trevîs, e a Cjamìn al Tiliment, come lûc da la anime dai siôrs trevisans.

'Professôr Brough, lui al à publicât une ricercje te universitât di Vicenze, '*The Ordeal of the da Camino, marquis in Treviso*"

'Pardabon? … Sì, cumò mi impensi.'

'Isal il so lavôr sui marchês trevisans intun ciert mût colegât ai fats contâts te tragjedie *Amlêt* di Shakespeare?'

'No rivi a capîlu, fantat, *distès a son plui robis in cîl e in tiere di chês insumiadis te nestre filosofie.*' Nol à ben capide la mê domande, ma distès cu la citazion dal *Amlêt* al clarìs il concet di trop limitadis e parziâls a sedin lis cognossincis dal om, parcè che al è limitât lui, tal so timp e tal so spazi.

'Professôr, te sô ricercje no aial speculât sul fat che la vere storie di *Amlêt* e podarès jessi sucedude in Italie, e fat riferiment al fratricidi di Riçart Second da Cjamìn?'

'Gjernazie tiraniche! No tu cjatis mai un brigant in dute Italie che nol sedi un perfet ligjere.'

Forsi o sin a bon. Il professôr si impense da la sô ricercje sui marchês da Cjamìn, e te frase dal *Amlêt* al scambie la Danimarche cu la Italie. Isal dome un lapsus Freudian, o ben cuant che si pense a laris e delincuents, si pense subit a la puare Italie? Distès, e vâl la pene di insisti par viodi se al ven fûr alc altri. No pensi che il president, cundut il

Comitât pal Amlêt Furlan, di sô iniziative si sedi inventât dut. Un storic al varà ben scuviert che inte Etât di Mieç nol risulte che un re o un nobil danês al vedi copât il fradi par cjapâ il podê e sposâ la femine. Situazion che magari si è verificade te Marcje trevisane. Po stâi che il professôr o cualchidun altri studiôs al vedi puartât i nobii trevisans come esempli par ilustrâ la depravazion dal podê di chei timps.

'Mister Brough, pensial che la frase di Marcello tal *Amlêt*, *'Alc 'l è lât frait tal stât da la Danimarche'*, sedi una frase gjeneriche che e podeve di sigûr lâ ben ancje pe Italie, pe Ingletiere, e pal fraidum istituzionâl e morâl dal mont intîr di in chê volte?'

'Sì, sì … Cemût che al va chest mont, tu cjatis une persone oneste su dîs mil,' al pant il professôr cun buine luciditât.

Di sigûr nol convente scomodâ Shakespeare, no covente une fantasime saltade fûr di une tombe par dînus che chest mont nol somee altri che une pucelente e schifose concentrazion di vapôrs.

Ancje se la situazion si è avonde sclaride, o provi a viodi se dal so lavôr, *'The Ordeal of the da Camino'*, al salte fûr cualchi element pal president dal Comitât. Tal câs che al vueli vê indaûr i bêçs dal gno viaç a Londre.

'Professôr, oltri al suspiet che il marchês Riçart Secont al sedi stât copât di so fradi Guecellon, e je ancje la pussibilitât che une biele femine, Giovannina Visconti, sposade cun Riçart, e podarès vê vude une part tal omicidi.' O cîr di tirâ fûr cualchi cantin dal so libri par stiçâ il so interès.

'No savìn. E jere la sô seconde compagne, femine di une impuartante famee di Pise, laudade di Dante Alighieri.'

'Tal so lavôr al à scrit che Dante Alighieri, tal Cjant IX dal Paradîs, nus conte dal omicidi di Riçart, nomo?'

'Sì, sì … carpir si fa la ragna … come a dî che Riçart sal spietave. Al leve indenant cul cjâf alt, ma nol saveve cui che al tramave cuintri di lui. Al steve zuiant a scacs tal so palaç, cuant che un sotan lu à colpît tal cjâf cuntune roncee.'

'Cuntune roncee!' Di sigûr, Shakespeare nol podeve doprâ un imprest cussì contadin par copâ un re. Disgotâ un velen intune orele al è fûr di dubi plui regâl.

'Professôr, podevie jessi la complicitât di Guecellon tal omicidi?' o torni a ribati cence grandis sperancis la teorie che mi à puartât culì fin a Londre.

'Cui pues savêlu? Lis vuardiis a àn copât il sassin. Forsi a volevin platâ alc. Cui puedial mai dîlu?' Brough al conferme il dubi dal pussibil fratricidi.

'E dove Sile e Cagnan s'accompagna, tal signoreggia e va con la testa alta, che già per lui carpir si fa la ragna,' il professôr al cite a memorie.

'Mi à dit che al è un insegnant, nomo? Cheste e je une citazion di Dante Alighieri! Al varès di cognossile.'

Mi rint cont che o sin rivâts insom, che il professôr Brough al à pierdude la pazience, e che di un moment a chel altri al podarès tornâ a jentrâ tal so mont paralêl fat di cidinôr e sbrocs improvîs di rabie e malcontent. Distès, o provi a rivâ a une conclusion cun lui.

'Professôr, lui al conferme che la fin di Riçart e je il risultât di une lote politiche, e no un complot al interni da la famee trevisane dai da Cjamìn. E l'*Amlêt* di Shakespeare nol à nuie a cefâ cun cheste facende,' i domandi in maniere retoriche.

'La tradizion e à une esistence simultanie e e compon un ordin simultani,' mi rispuint il professôr une vore ispirât. 'Il presint e il passât a esistin simultaneamentri. Ce che al sucêt cumò culì al è za sucedût di cualchi altre bande in

passât. Cui lu aial scrit?' Nus fisse di colp, stranît, par vê la rispueste che no rive. Dopo, al continue come un flum in plene viers la derive finâl.

'A son tantis lis robis che no cognossìn su Shakespeare. Parcè aial abandonât Stratford e la sô femine, Anne Hathaway? … Al à scugnût sposâle, vot agns plui vecje di lui, e cuntun frut tal grim … Pûr jê e à vivût plui a lunc. Lis feminis a son plui resistentis. La vendete di Lady Hathaway par la sô vite di artist fûr di cjase … I critics a disin che al è muart il dì dal so cincuantesimsecont complean. L'atôr di se stes, il puar comediant che si pavone, si remene une ore in sene … E ce dî da la dark lady dai sonets? Jerie une femine sposade o une zovine trative? … Oh, no rivi plui a stâ culì! Cumò o scuen lâ. Voaltris talians, adieu, adieu, int maraveose, mandolin e bon mangjâ … Sì, sì. O scuen lâ a cjase. Chest nol è il gno puest. Dulà ise la mê cjase? A drete o a çampe. O ai voie di viodi gno fi zimul, Hamnet! Dulà isal gno fi? Hamnet, parcè coristu vie di me? Fermaitlu! Fermaitlu … !'
Il professôr al cîr cun dificoltât di tirâsi sù di sentât. Nol è bon di bessôl, e la infermiere, che e je simpri stade sentade li in bande, e va svelte a judâlu.
'No sta tocjâmi! O scuen lâ a cjase! No sta tocjâmi!'
Ancje jo e Horatio si alcìn sù di sentâts par no jessi tirâts dentri dal batibui tra la infermiere e il professôr Brough.
Ducj nô o osservìn la situazion scaturîts.
'Chest nol è un paîs par vecjos. Un vecjo nol è altri che une robe misare, une robe teribile,' al murmuie Horatio tra se e se, cence fâsi sintî di mister Brough. Intant il professôr al continue il so personâl daidai cu la infermiere che e cîr di convincilu a tornâ a sentâsi cun nô, ma e finìs dome par iritâlu inmò di plui.
'Vie, va vie! Magari tu fossis avonde nete par spudâti

intor!' al busine a fuart.

In cheste teribile situazion jo o soi il plui espost, il plui umiliât dai events cussì inspietâts. O cîr il confuart di Horatio che al capìs la situazion, mi ven dongje e cu la sô vicinance al cîr di dâmi coragjo, cussì, di istint.

Nol à capît ben tancj passaçs da la conversazion, avonde oscure, tra me e il professôr. Al è stât spetadôr di une recite, un estrat di teatri dal assurt, dulà che il public nol sa se ridi o vaî pal compuartament ridicul e grotesc dai personaçs. A la fin ducj a restin in confusion. Al è come se a vessin viodût dentri di se il spieli dal lôr destin, e a vivin un sens di conturbie, di pôre, di ridicul. Horatio nol saveve nuie da la storie dai da Cjamìn, di Riçart Secont e so fradi Guecelon, ma al capive la impuartance che chei fats cussì lontans a vevin par me, e trop centrâl che al jere il professôr tes mês sperancis.

Al viôt il professôr Brough che si slontane cloteant, simpri parant vie la infermiere cuntune man. Cheste e cîr di sostignîlu parcè che al sbande, une vore malsigûr su lis gjambis. Chest fat lu irite inmò di plui. Nol acete il so aiût. Al vûl fâ di bessôl.

'Stupide di femine! La plui snorbeant misture di puce schifose che e vedi ufindût il nâs. O ai voie di lâ a cjase! Culì nol è il gno puest. La mê cjase e je là jù insom dongje dal Tamigi ... Vie, mate! Ti pestarès se no infetàs lis mans!' al continue a ufindi la puare femine.

La infermiere e cîr di consolâlu cun peraulis dolcis:

'Sù mo! Sta bon! O sai che tu sês un brâf om.'

Cu la fuarce fisiche dai siei trente agns e rive a cjapâlu a bracet e a acompagnâlu a piçui pas viers la puarte. Cumò il professôr Brough le cjale dut confusionât. Nol sa dulà che al è e ce che al sta fasint. Al è come vignût fûr di un brut sium, e ubidient come un puierut al çampete dongje di jê.

Al somee cuasi vê agrât di jessi jentrât tal mont reâl, come stranît da la esperience che al à vivût in chei moments di matetât.

LA FIN DI UN SIUM

O cjali impotent dute la sene, il çavariâ dal professôr, la sô
pierdite di cussience, di contat cul mont reâl.

'Chest nol è un paîs par vecjos,' al torne a dî Horatio cun
avilizion e frustrazion cjalant il professôr che si strissine
viers la puarte. 'Un vecjo al è un capot peçotôs picjât
suntun baston,' al ripet come une litanie. O sbat il cjâf a la
riflession amare di Horatio, intant che il professôr al è
rivât a la puarte e al abandone la sene.

Un altri sium che si sfante, une stele avostane che e cole
lontan. Dut inutil. Nol è nuie ce sperâ. Un vecjo nol è altri
che un capot peçotôs picjât suntun baston, se il so spirt nol
bat lis mans e al cjante a fuart, e plui fuart al cjante par
ogni sbrendul dal so vecjo capot mortâl.

Inutil, dut inutil. O ai crodût a la invenzion dal president
dal Comitât, forsi sugjestionât da la figure di Amlêt,
leterarie o reâl, di chel zovin sparît dal paîs e bintar in zîr
pal mont.

Intant, Amlêt al è inmò li sentât di bessôl. Si è puartât lis
mans su lis orelis par no sintî il vosâ dal professôr, 'cheste
no je cjase mê, chest nol è il gno puest', come cjapât dentri
di un deliri interiôr, i voi fis denant di se, concentrât
suntune vôs che i busine a fuart di cirî un puest dulà
platâsi, di scjampâ di chest mondat che al bruse. Miôr fâle
finide cun cheste vitace. Une sdramassade fin par tiere, e il
çocâ dal cerviel prime lent, tun, tun, tun, dopo simpri plui
fuart, e dopo il scjafoiâsi tal scûr.

E la int e pense che no tu sês tant a puest. Disêtmi une
peraule di confuart. O volarès tabaiâ cun gno pari, picjât
come un salam sot i trâfs da la tieze. No soi rivât a spiegâi
lis mês resons. No mi à dât il timp di dîsi che no jere colpe

mê se no i ubidivi, se no cumbinavi nuie a scuele. Al è alc che nol funzione tal gno cjâf. Un sunsûr continui, un murmui di vôs che a rivin di lontan. Tu âs di fâle finide. Vonde! Vonde!

O intuìs la situazion di conturbie di Amlêt.

'Amlêt, mi sintistu? Isal alc che o pues fâ, dâti une man, fâ alc par te?' i domandi.

I voi dongje par confuartâlu come un pari. Lu cjapi par une man, je strenç, e dopo cun chê altre lu tiri sù di sentât, dulà che al è restât fer, imobil, par dut il timp. Amlêt al è come un pês muart che al è jentrât intun mont di ombris dulà che nissun i vûl ben, nissun lu considere.

'Chest professôr culì mi fâs pôre,' mi dîs sustât. 'Mi fâs pensâ a la fantasime di gno pari che mi insumii simpri di gnot. Si presente cul non di Riçart da Cjamin, ma jo i dîs tu no tu sês gno pari, o soi il fi dal mulinâr insom da la roste. Intal sium lui al continue a dîmi che so fradi Guecelon lu à copât. E parcè ti varessial copât? Al veve pôre dal gno fi bastart, di te, Amlêt! Ma impensiti, impensiti … tu tu sês l'unic vêr erêt. Culì mi dismôf tal gno jet, dut sudât e sturnît.'

'Amlêt, chest sium che tu mi âs contât nol è altri che une invenzion da la tô ment stressade, malapaiade e avilide, come la mê cumò,' i dîs. 'Tu âs di tornâ tal mont reâl. Vonde fantasimis ta la tô esistence. Tu âs di preseâ il ben da la vite, frontâ lis situazions cun spirt positîf. Nol sarà facil, ma insiemi o vin di dâsi dentri, cun coragjo e determinazion.'

Amlêt al continue a cjalâ la puarte di dulà che al è jessût il professôr. Inçussît tai siei pinsîrs, al somee di no vê sintude une peraule di ce che i ai dit. Forsi la lezion di otimisim nol è un valôr che o rivi a trasmeti in chest moment, cu la disperazion dal gno enesim faliment che mi branche il cûr.

Restâts di bessôi ta la penombre da la sale, Horatio al è l'unic in grât di cjatâ une soluzion imediade, puartânus fûr dal ospizi e viodi insiemi se al è dut finît cul professôr, o se e je restade une sperance. Lu cjali come in spiete di un segnâl, di une reazion. Vino di lâ fûr di chi e indulà? Cuissà se al è inmò pussibil tabaiâ cul professôr la volte che si è calmât. Mai disperâ fin tal ultin, fin a la ultime silabe dal timp assegnât. Forsi doman al podarès sclarî alc da la sô publicazion sui marchês di Trevîs. Spiegânus cemût che secont lui Shakespeare al podarès jessi vignût a cognossince dai fats dai nobii da Cjamìn par scrivi l'*Amlêt*, o pûr smentî ogni colegament e definî i doi fats completamentri isolâts un di chel altri. Nancje trop rârs ta la storie da la umanitât di Cain in ca, l'omicidi dal fradi pal podê, par une femine, par la ereditât e v.i.

'O pensi che cumò o vin di lâ fûr dal ospizi,' mi dîs Horatio a basse vôs.

Lu cjali une vore avilît, no bon di cjatâ une soluzion.

'O sugjerìs di lâ tal gno ostel, dulà che o lavori e dulà che mi àn dât un sotet,' mi dîs. 'O podìn gustâ li.'

'Oh, gracie. O soi une vore grât!'

Dopo vê acetât di cûr l'invît di Horatio, il gno prin pinsîr al è par Amlêt.

'Nus invide a gustâ dulà che al lavore. Amlêt, vegnistu ancje tu?' i domandi.

Amlêt nol sint. Nol è in grât di capîmi in chest moment di turbament.

'Sigûr che tu vegnis cun nô!' lu confuarti.

'Il puest al è il Phoenix Hostel. Nol è lontan,' nus spieghe Horatio.

'Horatio, si racomandìn a te. In chest moment, jo e il gno amì culì no sin tal estri di decidi nuie.'

Si inviin par lâ fûr dal ospizi tun cidinôr che al cope.
Nissun di saludâ, nissun di ringraciâ, nissun par domandâ
se al è inmò pussibil tornâ a viodi il professôr, cul personâl
ridot al minim par vie da la crisi.
Horatio al è usât a cjaminâ par Londre. Da râr al cjape un
autobus o un tren.
'O nin a pît fin là. Va ben? Sêso in stât di cjaminâ?' nus
domande.
'Sigûr.'
'Mi plâs cjaminâ,' al zonte Horatio. 'Il miò Diu al è il Diu
dai cjaminadôrs. Se o cjaminais avonde a lunc,
probabilmentri no us covente un altri Diu.'
Ce isal miôr di torzeonâ par Londre, pes grandis citâts? Tu
ti sintis libar, tu ti fermis a cjalâ, a pensâ, e no dome il to
cuarp, ma ancje il to spirt al è content.
Al scuen jessi alc tal nestri cerviel che nus sburte a
cjaminâ dilunc lis stradis dal mont. La curiositât di cirî in
altrò un mont diferent, plui biel, plui just, e l'esperience
dal cjaminâ e je plene di aspietativis, e fâs part dal mont
dai siums e no tu sintis la fature, lis gjambis si movin
libaris e il puest di arîf al è dome une tape intermedie dal
viaç finâl. Il nestri percors al va dret viers la mete
bramade, la montagne incjantade, Shangri-La, la isule da
la nestre fantasie, la utopie dai nestris desideris plui
scuindûts, la idee di rivâ intun puest ideâl dulà fermâsi e
costruî alc e lassâ un segn, un ricuart, par chei che dopo di
nô passant par li a condividaran la stesse sodisfazion, la
nestre gjonde viers la vite.
*Cence di me par miârs di agns il garofolâr al sarà dut un
butul e la vierte e sflorirà, ma chei che in segret e àn capît
il gno cûr a vignaràn dongje a visitâ la tombe dulà ch'o
stoi.* Ma il cjamin ti pues ancje puartâ di montagne in
montagne, cence une destinazion finâl, ae continue

ricercje di alc di gnûf, une smanie di cognossince par lis
stradis dal mont.

Cui varaial imparât di plui da la vite, chei che a son lâts sù
e jù par montagnis e a traviers i mârs cence un pont di arîf,
o pûr chei che une volte rivâts insom da la val incjantade a
àn fissât la lôr dimore e metudis lidrîs?

O cjapi a bracet Amlêt cuntun contat delicât, dome a
cjareçâ il braç. Amlêt mi ven daûr strissinant il so cuarp
indenant, cence vigôr, cence fuarce. Fûr da la struture si
inviin daûr di Horatio par stradutis che dome lui al cognòs.
La zornade si va un fregul fuscant, e à pierdût il sflandôr
estîf da la matine. Cuant che o passìn denant da la glesie di
Saint Mary, il cjampanili al bat lis dôs dopomisdì. Un colp
sec che mi lasse come sopendût par un atim, un moment di
riflession, di conturbie. I nestris minûts a corin svelts viers
la fin.

DOS DOPOMISDÌ A CJAMÌN

L'orloi dal cjampanili da la Glesie di Ognissant a Cjamìn al Tiliment al bat lis dôs dopomisdì, cuant che Carmela si dismôf. Distirade sul jet, e cjale la lûs che e jentre par lis fressuris da la persiane. Difûr al è plen dì. Il so prin pinsîr al va al diretôr, al so gnûf amôr: cuarp salt, ... jesus ... di sierâ i voi e tirâ un biel respîr … gjoldi la vite. Mi fâs sintî plui femine, plui considerade. Guglielmo nol è cussì. Chel biât di om al podeve almancul telefonâ … ce i costavie? Nuie. Al è fat cussì. Miôr stâ di bessôl par evitâ i fastidis. Miôr rinunciâ a vivi par no vê rognis. Ma jo no ai inmò cuarante agns e no mi rassegni, no mi fermi. No mi soi mai fermade te vite. Al è come se o ves vivût cetantis vitis diferentis. Cuant che o ai nasât che alc nol leve, mi soi subite diliberade di chel pês.

Tantis vitis, ma une sole di fat, e no viôt parcè che cumò no varès di gjoldile che o soi tal plen dal istât. Cogli l'attimo, seize the day, se cun Guglielmo nol funzione plui, o vin di cirî ce che al è biel e positîf in chest moment, cence fâ cont che doman al larà miôr, che doman dut si justarà … Balis! Nol è cussì. Mi plâs sintî l'om dongje che mi da impuartance. Mi plâs sintî une spale fuarte che mi da sostegn, saponte. Tu âs di dâ al om la aparince che lui al à la iniziative, al decît lis robis par te, par vêlu ae fin ai tiei pîts. Cun Guglielmo un jet frêt. Forsi, viodìn, no sai, e mai un sì, sì, sì. Mil indecisions, e nol è cussì che tu fasis contente une femine. No come chel altri, il gno diretôr. Usgnot mi fermi a durmî li di lui. No lu vevi mai fat di cuant che o ai cognossût Guglielmo, ma si cambie vele. Vai dove ti porta il vento. Lui a Londre a cirî fortune e jo cul gno diretôr a fâ l'amôr.

Cuant che o fasìn l'amôr, mi acuarç che al è dut gno, dispost a fâ dut par me. In chel totâl abandon mi sint come murî, e o volarès chei moments a durassin par simpri, al infinît. Une droghe che mi fâs stâ ben, mi jude. Moments che mi coronin la regjine dal creât, uniche. A son dute la mê vite. O deventi la mari di un mont gnûf.

Soi une puare femine, lu amet, ma chei moments mi dan sostance, coragjo, mi judin a tirâ indenant, a acetâ lis sdramassadis che la vite ti risierve, parcè che mi sint dentri la fuarce di une mantide che e cree e distruç, e da la vite e la muart, parone dal so destin.

Dopo la muart dal piçul, Guglielmo al à fermât di vivi. Jo invezit no mi fermi mai, e la mê rabie mi fâs cori inmò plui svelte. O ai simpri pensât che bisugne dî shit, shit, shit, cuant che lis robis no funzionin, e no Diu ca, Diu là. Sta cul om che ti fâs stâ ben, che al è dispost a dâti dut … fin cuant che al dure, dopo al è un altri dì e si viodarà.

GUSTÂ AL PHOENIX HOSTEL

Il Phoenix Hostel al è la tipiche struture brownstone cun modons a viste, su doi plans, grancj barcons cun telârs blancs, malsestâts, che si tirin sù e jù a ghiliotine. Al ingrès, al è un sens di precarietât, pôc si paie e pôc si gjolt, ma ancje di alternatîf che al ven dal personâl informâl cui ospits, dai mûrs tapezâts di posters, fotos, invîts, informazions dai events in citât, e da la atmosfere cun tante int zovine che si salude, si ferme vulintîr par une tabaiade, o pûr pal sempliç gust di stâ insiemi. A pene jentrâts, si capìs subite che Horatio al è une presince familiâr, une persone considerade e une vore ben volude pe sô culture, pal so fâ cortês e rispietôs di ducj. Ancje Amlêt in chel ambient vivarôs al è tornât a vê un pôc di snait, di fiducie, e al cjale curiôs chel mont familiâr che inte vite, e in particolâr tai ultins mês, nol à mai vivût.
Horatio nus acompagne intune grande sale cun poltronis e sofàs che a àn cognossût i doi conflits mondiâi, plenis di zovins che si tirin un toc in bande par fânus un pôc di puest. Jo e Amlêt o cjatìn di sentâsi su dôs poltronutis dongje dal barcon, invezit Horatio si sente sul divan dongje di une biele frutine di colôr sui dîs, undis agns, che si e strente par lassâi un pôc di spazi, e lu cjale cun vivôr, mostrant l'amôr che si à viers un pari. Dopo si vicine a lui, come par cirî l'afiet di une cjarece. O cjali dute la sene cun curiositât. O provi un fregul di imbaraç a cjatâmi cun chê compagnie zovine di dutis lis etniis e culturis, e jo, dongje dai cincuante, cuasi il plui vecjo. Horatio, su la sessantine, mi è di confuart, mi fâs sintî mancul di bessôl, ancje se al somee movisi in chel mont di zoventût cu la disinvolture di un adolessent.

La sale dulà che si sin sentâts e comuniche, par un passaç
sot di un arc, cu la cusine di dulà che al rive un ticâ di
plats, e un sù e jù di zovins che a van a cjoli alc tal frigo.
No si rivin a viodi i fornei, ma si pues imagjinâ che
cualchidun al sta cusinant alc dal profum di mangjâ che al
rive fintremai tal salot.
'Vino di gustâ culì? O ai tacos di poleç tal frigo,' nus dîs
Horatio.
Al fâs il paron di cjase, e al ufrìs ce che al à disponibil
intal frigo comun dal ostel. O sai di jessi inmò in debit da
la gulizion, e par indole no soi usât a profitâ. O propon di
lâ a comprâ alc intun piçul supermarcjât che o vin passât
par rivâ tal ostel.
'O sês miei ospits. Al è mangjâ za pront, sempliç di
scjaldâ tal microondis. Nissun fastidi!' mi dîs Horatio.
'Mi plasarès judâ, contribuî in cualchi mût ...' i spieghi il
gno fastidi.
'Al pues lâ a cjoli cualchi bire tal bar, se lui e il so amì no
sês astemis … Mi plasarès un pocje bire, e lui?'
'Va ben, perfet.'
Par solit jo no bêf bire, ma mi somee une buine soluzion, e
mi alci sù par lâ a ordenâ lis biris al bar che si cjate inta la
sale plui dongje da la jentrade dal ostel. Impins par spietâ
il gno turni, o viôt un zovin che mi osserve cun interès. Su
la trentine, biel aspiet curât, cjavei curts e ordenâts,
bregonuts firmâts e clark cence cjalçuts, alc di diferent di
chei altris ospits.
'O sês talians, nomo?' mi domande il zovin.
'Cemût âstu fat a capîlu?'
'Tu sâs, cui talians no si sbalie. O sarìn un pôc superficiâi,
ma di sigûr creatîfs. La 'biele figure' e fâs part da la nestre
nature. Se o podìn permetisal, o spindìn e o curìn il nestri
aspiet plui di chei altris.'

'O soi dacuardi … Di dulà sêstu?'
'Di Spoleto.'
'In visite a Londre?'
'No propit. O ai une lauree in architeture, ma in Italie cjatâ lavôr par ce che tu âs studiât al è simpri plui un miraç.'
'Un cerviel in fughe? Ae ricercje di un lavôr in Ingletiere?'
'Sì e no. O stoi seguint un master sul moviment da lis Arts and Crafts di William Morris. Forsi no tu lu cognossis, ma al è un argoment che mi à simpri inmagât …'
'Dôs bitters e une lager. Dîs sterlinis e cincuante,' al busine il barist, e al poie trê bocâi di bire sul banc. O tiri fûr dal tacuin un biliet di dîs sterlinis. Un dai ultins. No pues fâ di mancul di pensâ che la mê setemane a Londre e je in pericul se no rivi a controlâ lis spesis.
'Sint mo, no si sin presentâts. Mi clami Giuliano.'
'Guglielmo.'
'Guglielmo, parcè no preparìno une buine pastesute? O insegnìn a chescj culì cemût che si prepare. Ir o ai viodût i todescs che a butavin dentri i spaghets ta la aghe frede!' mi conte cuntune ridade sardoniche.
'Va ben, nô o sin in trê là jù insom, se nol è di trop disturp.'
'La passade di pomodoro, dôs ulivis e paste trop che al covente. Par un o par cuatri si sporcje une sole pignate.'
'Va ben, ma o vuei contribuî su la spese. O visi i miei amîs e o ordini une bire ancje par te. Okay?'
'Sigûr.'
O cjapi sù lis biris dal banc e mi invii viers la sale dulà che no viôt plui Horatio. Lis poi jù sul taulin denant di Amlêt che no si è mot da la poltrone. Pierdût tal so mont, al trabascje alc par so cont, tirant su di se la atenzion da la frute di front che lu cjale fis un fregul preocupade.
'Amlêt, dulà isal Horatio?' i domandi.

Cuntun mot dal cjâf al indiche viers la cusine dulà che si rive a olmâlu, dut impegnât a scjaldâ i tacos di poleç tal microondis. O voi viers la cusine dulà che al è un mismàs di altris zovins indafarâts: cualchidun al mangje une bocjade impins, altris a lavin i plats tal lavel o a tegnin a ments alc che al bol ta la pignate. Horatio al è ocupât cui siei tacos.

'Horatio, o ai cognossût un zovin talian tal bar. Forsi tu lu cognossis ancje tu. Si è ufiert di preparâ une pastesute par ducj nô. Insiemi.' Lu informi dal incuintri cun Giuliano.

'Sì. Benon. Alore spaghets e tacos. O varìn un gustâ complet.'

In chel al rive in cusine il talian cui spaghets, e dut ce che al covente par fâ une pastesute al pomodoro. Al è li tal ostel di cualchi setemane, e al à za vût mût di scambiâ cualchi peraule cun Horatio, che lu salude a pene lu viôt. Si met subit al lavôr, e al dimostre di cognossi ben il puest e ancje di vê une cierte abilitât ai fornei. O resti impins dongje di lui, pront a dâ une man se al covente.

GJENERAZIONS A CONFRONT

Al è naturâl in similis situazions, cuant che si fâs la cognossince di un zovin talian tal forest, di tacâ a tabaiâ da la Italie, dai principâi fats politics e sociâi, dai cambiaments sucedûts tai ultins mês.

'No tornarai plui in Italie. Garantît! Pluitost mi met a lavâ plats, cualsisei lavôr culì a Londre,' mi pant Giuliano.

'Al sarès util che i zovins a restassin in Italie, no pensistu? Par cambiâ lis robis ...'

'In Italie lis robis no cambiaràn mai. I zovins a son avilîts, e la plui part no crôt che al sedi pussibil cjatâ un lavôr, fâ une vite normâl, sposâsi e meti sù famee ...'

'Cjalant la mê situazion di cumò no mi sint di dâti tuart, ancje se o soi di une altre gjenerazion. Ma cuant che o vevi la tô etât, nol jere cussì.'

'Lu sai, la crisi politiche dai agns setante e novante, la contestazion tes universitâts e la lote tes fabrichis ... Gno pari mi à ben istruît su chês robis.'

'Propit, mi dismenteavi che tu podaressis jessi gno fi. E to pari un gno coscrit. Ma ancje par me al è dut cambiât cumò. Crodimi!'

Fin a la etât di chest fantat culì, il sens di apartignince a un partît politic di sinistre lu colegavi a dut ce che al jere zovin, vivarôs, inteligjent, intraprendent. Ma za in chê volte, vie pes cjaminadis solitariis in mont, mi fermavi a cjalâ lis cimis sblancjadis di nêf che si alçavin tal cîl turchin, e o pensavi che lis montagnis a jerin li di milions di agns, e su chei stes crets, prime di me, si jerin rimpinâts i oms primitîfs, e prime di lôr formis di vite sparidis par simpri. E la sere o levi a cjaminâ par la campagne, a rimirâ il cîl stelât, e o pensavi al spazi infinît dal univers, dulà che la stele plui dongje, la Proxima Centauri, e je lontane cuatri agns lûs, miliarts e miliarts di chilometris, e ce che o viodìn cumò cui nestris telescopis, al è un mont che al esisteve milions di agns indaûr.

Pensant a dut chest, l'om si spaurìs, e al medite su trop relatîfs che a son i nestris sfuarçs par cambiâ il mont, considerant la nestre breve esistence, la nestre nature crevadice, trop limitâts che o sin tal timp e tal spazi. Cuant che tu cjalis la furmiute che e cor di bessole sù par la mont, o daûr di miârs di altris furmiutis che tu 'nt tibiis no sai tropis cence savê, tu ti domandis cemût che e je finide fin là sù, e cuâl isal il so intindiment. Almancul chês che o ai jo tal ort a coltivin i pedoi sui zermois dai cudumars, a àn alc cefâ, ancje se a cumbinin disastris, e cuntune sborfade di velen int copi miârs. Gas! Gas! Un daspâ salvadi. Sino cussì ancje nô? L'evoluzion dal caos che al è l'univers.

E cussì, la politiche, la economie, la passion che i metevi tal fâ lis robis pensant che a sedin par simpri, che a sedin eternis, un pôc a la volte a son smamidis, si son riveladis une ilusion, come dute la nestre sience, lis invenzions e v. i. L'univers al è indiferent al nestri travai, aes nestris concuistis economichis e sociâls, ai nestris sfuarçs par cambiâ il mont.

'Cuant che o vevi la tô etât, il pinsîr da la sinistre al jere un credo che la plui part dai zovins a condividevin. A jerin tantis sperancis, e la idee di podê cambiâ il mont dentri di un partît e someave une realtât pussibile. E dopo …' no rivi a finî il resonament che Giuliano mi interomp.

'E dopo intune realtât simpri plui globâl si sês cjatâts plui vecjos, e il mont che al leve te direzion contrarie a chê sperade. La stesse litanie che o ai sintût no sai tropis voltis dai miei gjentôrs.'

'Eh sì. Un brut sveâsi.'

O ai començât a pensâ al ingjan di chês cunvignis di politiche a cjacarâ di int che no cognossevin. 'Compagni' di chê altre bande dal mont che o varessin volût liberâ da la sclavitût, preocupâts da la lôr miserie, da la lôr infelicitât.

E par cirî la felicitât di chei altris, no sin stâts plui bogns di vê a cûr la nestre felicitât. La incapacitât di gjoldi da lis robis semplicis che la vite nus risierve. La politiche, l'impegn sociâl nus puartavin a considerâ dome il futûr di un mont globâl, invezit di vivi la realtât atuâl che o vin dongje di nô.

O ai començât a pensâ che il gno leam a une ideologjie di partît, il totâl impegn politic mi devin un sens di disasi. La convinzion che o stevi pierdint il gno timp in fufignis mi à fat considerâ la idee di vê une famee mê, cuntun frut di cressi che ti cor ator, che al à dut ce imparâ. O jeri une vore confondût. La prioritât e je deventade di cjatâ un lavôr, l'amôr da la femine, la compagnie di un fi. Ma il fi nol è vignût, e l'amôr par la mê femine al è lât pôc a pôc smamintsi. E mi rint cont che la idee di jessi part di une comunitât, di vivi insiemi esperiencis, progjets no esistin plui ta la mê vite. Mi sint di bessôl, cence ideis, cence la voie di tornâ a partî.

Ancje cumò, cuant che o cjali lis montagnis che si iluminin tal soreli di prime matine, mi ven di pensâ che lôr a son li di milions di agns, e nô, cu lis nestris vitis cussì curtis di passion e dolôr, no sin nuie. E o resti cidin a osservâ lis montagnis che si inflamin al calâ dal soreli.

Nuie. Nuie cefâ.

'Puedio domandâti … simpri se no ti secje, ce che tu fasis culì a Londre,' mi domande Giuliano bot e sclop.

Cemût spiegâi la mê situazion, il motîf da la mê presince

culì a Londre, a un zovin che al sburte pal cambiament, che al confide inmò su la inteligjence da la int?

Nol podarà mai capîlu. Soredut un fantat di cjâf che al cjale cun suspiet, cun sens critic, la gjenerazion dai siei gjenitôrs che e à creât un sisteme blocât, dulà che il passaç di testimoni al è deventât impussibil. Ai zovins ur ven dineade la sperance, il just ricognossiment sociâl. A une persone preparade come chest zovin culì, il provincialisim, la superficialitât, la ignorance che a àn puartât un nuie come me fin chi a Londre, i somearès une cjapade pal cûl, la ironie di un mont malât.

'Mi cjati a Londre par intervistâ un professôr universitari in pension, un critic di Shakespeare che al à insegnât par tancj agns in Italie,' i rispuint cuntune cierte esitazion.

'Ti paie la universitât o ise une tô iniziative personâl?' mi domande.

'Mi dan alc … Al è ancje un gno interès personâl,' i dîs cirint di platâ la bausie.

'Ancje jo o ai cirût di fâ alc cu la universitât di Perugia, ma il sisteme al jere cussì blocât, e bêçs e progression di cariere cuasi impussibii … O ai rinunciât.'

Giuliano si zire par viodi da la paste, e il discors al cole lì, cence la vergogne di spiegâi che o soi inmò un insegnant precari, e che o ziri di scuele in scuele, li che mi mandin. Situazion che o vîf cun frustrazion e o cîr di platâ, ancje se mi lasse dentri simpri un malstâ dificil di paidî.

'Jo chi o varès finît. La pastesute e je pronte. Prove a viodi dai plats e da lis possadis, se al à za pensât Horatio …'

'Lu ai viodût che lu steve fasint.'

'Okay. Alore judimi a scolâ la paste. Chescj inglês no cognossin il colepaste. e o vin di rangjâsi in cualchi mût.' mi dîs Giuliano cuntune ridade sarcastiche.

Ator da la taule, tal cjanton plui lontan da la sale, Horatio al ten sù la compagnie. Sentât in mieç tra Amlêt e la frute, al sta contant alc di divertent. Ducj a ridin contents. Un moment di solêf dopo lis delusions da la matinade. Su chê taule nol mancje propit nuie: i plats cu la paste, i tacos, lis biris, e i voi di chê frutine che a riducin contents. Fin Amlêt al mostre plui estri, e chê compagnie legre i fâs bon pro. Horatio al fâs di paron di cjase, e al à volût ricreâ la atmosfere familiâr, di condivision, che si cjate par solit tai ostei.

Al ven a sentâsi dongje di me. Al sa di dovê une spiegazion su la frutine di colôr che si è sentade cun nô. Giuliano no i à badât a chel plat in plui su la taule, e ducj a somein gjoldi da la ligrie che il bon mangjâ al à puartât, cence fastidis.

Distès, Horatio i ten a sclarî ai siei amîs talians la gnove dimension di se che al à cjatât tal ostel. Culì, al à volût meti a disposizion di chei altris la sô cognossince da la nature umane, la sô esperience di om navigât che al à zirât il mont. Dopo tant viazâ di un puart a chel altri, l'ostel al rapresente la sô cjase. Al conte dal incuintri cu la frute che i sta dongje. Un incuintri salvific che al dimostre che judant lis personis che a son in dibisugne, tu judis ancje te stes.

'A pene rivât in chest ostel za fa sîs, siet agns, e jere cheste frutine sordemute, si clame Abidal, juste abandonade di sô mari. La puare femine e veve scugnût lassâ il paîs, jessint in Ingletiere ilegalmentri, e acusade di spaç di droghe.' Horatio nus conte cun passion.

'La uniche pussibilitât che la frute e veve di restâ culì e jere di separâle da la mari. Chê volte e veve cinc agns, a pene tacade scuele. Cussì jo o ai decidût di ocupâmi di jê, in afidament. O soi il so nono adotîf, e cumò jê mi vûl tant ben. E je deventade une brave frute. O speri che prime o dopo sô mari e vigni a cjolile. Jo o soi simpri chi, il so nonut.' Horatio nus spieghe cun emozion.

La frute e intuìs che Horatio al à tabaiât di jê, e si tire dongje di lui cundut l'amôr e l'afiet che e pues mostrâ pal om che le jude a cressi.

Jo e Giuliano o vin seguît cun atenzion la confession di Horatio, e le condividin cun bielis peraulis di incoragjament. La sô sielte, la promesse fate a la mari di viodi di jê fin cuant che e tornarà a Londre, e comôf ducj nô.

Mi cjati denant dal esempli di une filosofie che o ai simpri cjarinât: di volê ben a chei che ti stan dongje, condividi cun lôr i biei ricuarts, la felicitât, ma ancje il profont dolôr e i displasês, parcè che il mont al continuarà par la sô strade, e dome chei moments a saran impuartants dopo dut. Cul lâ indenant dal timp ancje chei sintiments a laran simpri al macul, fin a sparî dal dut cun nô, cuant che o deventarìn vecjos e o murirìn.

Filosofiis, sistemis morâi, ideologjiis a son come spicis di montagnis fûr dai nûi, viodudis a une grande distance, nissune plui alte, plui impuartante, plui vere di chês altris, ma la vite e je ca jù, cun chei che ti vuelin ben e ti stan dongje.

Dopo il biel gustâ in compagnie, al rive il moment dai cumiâts, che se par Horatio e Giuliano al vûl dî tornâ a la normalitât da la vite di ogni dì, par me, invezit, e reste la amarece dal enesim faliment, ven a stâi, la cuistion da la mê visite a Londre a la ricercje dal professôr Brough e da lis provis sul Amlêt furlan. Dut cuant si è rivelât fake news come ch'o vevi pôre.

Dopo vê saludât Giuliano e vê scambiât cun lui vicendevui auguris di sucès professionâl, e bon pro pe puare Italie disgraciade, o resti impins denant di Horatio, dal gno amì inglês, indecîs su ce fâ. Dome un moment, parcè che Horatio mi cjape une man e me strenç cun calôr. Si capìs che nol è stât un incuintri ocasionâl, che o varessin tantis altris robis di dîsi, ma la vite ti puarte a continuâ il cjamin, cu la cjame di responsabilitâts che ognidun di nô si puarte daûr. A Horatio i son bastadis lis pocjis oris di compagnie par capî il gno caratar, la mê dificoltât, il faliment da la mê imprese a Londre.

'Se i covente il gno aiût doman, jo o soi chi. O podìn provâ a tornâ a viodi il professôr Brough,' mi dîs Horatio.

'No sai, Horatio,' i dîs perplès.

'La demence senîl e à moments di salustri.'

'Sì, ma distès o soi plen di dubis,' i esprim il gno seticisim sul rinsavî dal professôr.

'O capìs, ma cumò o sin amîs, e tu sâs dulà che o soi a stâ, e … se al covente …'

'Gracie, Horatio. Tu sês un vêr amì.'

'Oh, di nuie,'

Horatio al va par saludâ Amlêt che al è simpri restât sentât a taule, jentrât tal so mont paralêl. Al à tirâts sù i zenoi su la cjadree e al murmuie alc tra se e se, la viste suntun rai di lûs che al jentre dal barcon viert. Sentade denant, la piçule sordemute e cjale il zovin cun interès, e al pâr che e vedi capît la clâf di ingrès dal mont di Amlêt, il fîl dai siei pinsîrs, tal cidinôr dal so mont silenziôs.

Horatio nol sa nuie dai problemis di Amlêt, e nol à nancje ben capît ce che nus ten insiemi. Al cîr la man dal zovin par saludâlu, ma Amlêt nol capìs, nol sint, no i bade. Alore Horatio i da juste une pacute suntune spale che lu fâs scatâ sù di colp e stacâsi di lui, come se al ves viodût il diaul in persone.

I voi dongje, lu cjapi a bracet, e saludant la compagnie, lu acompagni fûr dal ostel cun dute la delicatece che i vûl.

Cuant che o sin di bessôi in strade, mi ven di pensâ al discors di Horatio, a la sô disponibilitât, al segn di amicizie che mi à mostrât, e o sint dentri di me che alc al sta cambiant. O sint fuarte la responsabilitât viers Amlêt, la vision di une altre vite, diferente, che Horatio mi à ben fat viodi cul so esempli.

DOPOMISDI' A LONDRE

L'orloi dal tor da la Christ Church of England su la Bell
Street al bat lis cinc dopomisdì. Il timp difûr al è cambiât,
e un aiar ledrôs al somee clamâ dongje un temporâl. No
sai ce fâ di precîs. Mi rint cont che no pues impegnâ
Horatio cu lis mês facendis personâls. O sai ancje di vê
une grande responsabilitât viers Amlêt. Chest impegn
morâl al devente simpri plui impuartant. E nol è dome
Amlêt che al à bisugne di me, ma e sta deventant une
cuistion reciproche. O sint dentri di me i beneficis da la sô
presince.
Cumò bisugne inventâ alc par vignî fûr da la situazion
ingredeade dulà che si cjatìn. Di istint, mi ricuardi che o
sin intun cuartîr che o cognossevi ben cuant che o lavoravi
a Londre, e mi ven voie di tornâ indaûr di vincj agns, a la
'swinging London' da la mê zoventût.
Parcè no mostrâ a Amlêt alc dai puescj che mi son cussì
familiârs, che o cognòs cussì ben, e condividi cun lui
ricuarts, emozions di une etât lontane, i miei timps da la
post lauree, cuant che o jeri in Ingletiere par sfrancjâ il gno
inglês? O vevi plui o mancul i agns di Amlêt cumò, e o
lavoravi intun pub a nord di Regent's Park, no lontan di
Hampstead, la zone plui biele di Londre. Mi viôt inmò
daûr il banc dal 'The George', cussì si clamave il pub, su la
Haverstock Hill, a dâ fûr bocâi di *lager* e *bitter and lime*.
Mi impensi inmò da la strade che tantis voltis o ai fat a pît
par lâ in centri, fin a Marble Arch, dilunc Belsize Grove,
Primrose Hill, Regent's Park. Biei timps! Il pub al è un pôc
lontan e i vûl cuasi une ore a pît. No sai se Amlêt al è usât
a cjaminâ cussì a lunc. La temperadure e je ideâl cul aiarin
che al à rinfrescjât il tart dopomisdì.

'Amlêt, vuelistu fâ une cjaminade cun me ta la Londre che o cognòs cussì ben?' i domandi.
Amlêt nol rispuint, ma mi ven daûr, e al somee di no vê alternativis.
'A son i lûcs dulà che o ai lavorât, cuant che o vevi la tô etât,' i conti cjaminant viers Park Road.
'I ricuarts a son ce che nus tegnin vîfs, cuant che o sin blocâts e no cjatìn la strade par lâ indenant …'
Al è un monolic, ma Amlêt mi sta a sintî e mi ven daûr cun bon pas.
La int che o incrosìn e torne di vore, in code denant da la fermade dai autobus, o di premure jù pes scjalis a cjapâ il tren da la metropolitane. Une ore o forsi plui par tornâ a cjase, ta la Grande Londre.
Un trop di int si sburte denant di un barachin sul marcjepît, par ingosâsi impins cuntun burger, une bocjade di dôs sterlinis. Altre int si cjate in code denant di un cine pai biliets dal spetacul in cartelon. Altre trupe e spiete di consumâ la ultime ilusion, the great hit, il conciert dal lôr idul intun locâl li dongje.
L'aiarin di sore sere al à parât vie i nûi dal temporâl, ma al à puartât dongje tante porcarie. Sacuts di plastiche, sfueis di gjornâl a svoletin par aiar prime di colâ jù suntun grun di scovacis, sot il riflès da lis lûs da la publicitât.
Une fantate bessole, sentade suntune bancjine dentri Regent's Park, e je dute cjapade cul so telefonut. E à voi smavîts, vaiulints, stracs di cjoche e strapàs. E da une cjalade a la int di passaç, ma no viôt nissun. Si cjape sù bessole e si incjamine viers cjase, il cjâf a pendolon, la muse stufadice, foreste a dut ce che i sta ator.

IL PUB 'THE GEORGE'

A son cuasi siet di sere cuant che dilunc la Primrose Hill Road si stin vicinant al pub, dulà che o ai lavorât par trê mês. 'The George', mal impensi ben, al jere un pôc diferent di chei altris pubs di Londre. Al veve plui lûs dentri e i barcons a lassavin viodi difûr. Parsore la puarte d'ingrès la insegne cu la scrite 'The George', cun dongje il dissen di une corone. Forsi in onôr dal re barbot, George VI, chel dal film cun Colin Firth. Un re che si è fat ben volê da la sô int intant da la seconde vuere mondiâl. E je simpri tante int impins difûr, istât e invier, par une babade sul balon o une pipade, cui bocâi da la bire poiâts sui caratei disponûts al ingrès. Des cuatri e mieze aes siet di sere, cu la Happy Hour, nol è puest dentri e nancje difûr, soredut cu la biele stagjon.

Cuant che o jentrìn, mi impensi subite dal tipic odôr da la bire spandude su la moquette. O voi tra i clients impins viers il banc. Amlêt mi ven daûr. O soi curiôs di viodi se al è inmò il gno vecjo paron, ma li no cognòs plui nissun. Mi disin che al à vendût il pub za fa dîs agns, e no san plui nuie di lui.

O conti di mangjâ une bocjade e stâ un moment in pâs, ma dentri nol è puest nancje impins. Inciert su ce fâ, o cjali Amlêt, striçât tra i clients che a tabain a plene vôs tal davoi dal puest. O soi li li par lâ fûr, cuant che dôs feminis, sentadis di bessolis intun cjanton dal locâl, nus fasin segn di comodâsi a la lôr taule.

No vin sielte. Nancje al banc tu cjatis puest par ordenâ. Si sentìn dongje da lis dôs zovinis inglesis. Amlêt, a man drete di une fantate in cjar, su la trentine, cuntune biele muse taronde, cjavei curts e riçots, curade tal vistîsi, la cotule atilade parsore i zenoi, e une t-shirt fantasie cun dôs pipinis in biele viste sul denant. E bevucje un gin tonic dongje a finîsi. La fantate sentade a la mê diestre e je un toc di zovine, ben spalade, ombui fuarts in biele evidence tai jeans aderents, une espression un tic biadine, la muse ordenarie contornade di cjavei luncs fin su lis spalis. E à denant di se une pinte di bire cuasi plene. Tu puedis scometi che no je la prime.

A ridin contentis, ma e je simpri la tarondute riçote a murmuiâ alc sot vôs, intant che chê altre, forsi za fate, si limite a sgagnî di stupidute. Si pues intuî che nô doi o sin al centri dai lôr discors.

Cuant che il camarîr nus ven dongje, o ordeni dôs pintis di lager cence pensâ sore. Forsi tal gno sub-cussient no vuei jessi di mancul di chês signorinis culì, o forsi tai miei ricuarts di camarîr dal locâl, par bevi dome mieze pinte tu sês propit malât. Mi impensi ancje che Amlêt nol à nancje tocjade la bire dal Phoenix Hostel. Un fat avonde strani se o pensi che in Friûl, prime di vignî vie, al beveve come une spugne. O noti ancje che il zovin, pôc usât a stâ dongje di une femine, al è li sentât dut impicotît, cu la cjaladure tal vueit denant di se. E nancje a fâlu a pueste, la zovine in scalmane si è vicinade par provocâlu un tininin.

'Talians? Oh! Mi plâs la Italie!' e dîs a fuart la riçotute, dopo che daûr da la lôr domande si sin presentâts.

'Al è un biel sogjet … il fantat,' e murmuie viers la compagne, cu la intenzion di fâsi sintî ancje di me. Cheste si limite a un ridi stupidut, concentrade su la bire. E somee çurule, in stât di capî lis robis dome a metât.

Amlêt si è metût a fissâ un bocon di om li dongje, cuntun bocon di stomi. Al sbisìe cun foghe su la slot, al da une manade sui veris colorâts par sbrocâ la fote. Nol pues començâ di gnûf. Al à voie di femine par slizerî il so marum. Al à olmât une fantate che al cognòs ben, sentade al banc. I va dongje, une man su la cuesse ben tornide fûr da la mini. Al à di mostrâ dute la sô vanitât. Jê lu cjale sturnide, e lui al profite da la sô indiference.

Al rive il camarîr cu lis biris. Pai burger bisugne spietâ. O mandi jù cualchi glutâr, ma Amlêt no si môf di sentât. Al sta dret come un pâl, mans sui zenoi, intimidît da lis avances da la riçotute che si è fate indenant cu la cjadree, il so cuarp cuasi a contat cun chel dal zovin. Lis mans che a corin libaris sul ôr da la cotule curte, sui zenoi, a lissâ i cjavei riçots, intune ande di fuarte seduzion. A pene che e incrose la mê cjalade, e torne in se, tirant di gnûf un pôc inlà la cjadree. Ancje la fantaçone dongje di me, pûr cun moviments lents e grivis, mi da une cjalade di sot coç in spiete di une reazion.

'Al è flap! … l'uciel si capìs … âstu viodût?' la riçotute e pant viers la compagne che si limite a riduçâ parsot. Il so intendiment al è di fâsi sintî di me par studiâ la mê reazion. A viodin che Amlêt al à alc che nol va.

'Al è cence passion … un toc di len …' Peraulis pandudis sot vôs viers la compagne, ma avonde fuart par fâsi sintî ancje di me.

Mi sint responsabil da la situazion di Amlêt, e no sai ce reazion che al podarès vê in chel moment di profonde confusion mentâl.

A son cuasi nûf di sere cuant che a fuarce di vitis a rivin i burgers. Mi met a mangjâ dopo vê dade une biele clucade di bire. Amlêt nol tocje il burger, al reste fer, inclaudât a la cjadree, une vore turbât.

No mi sint di saborâ chê situazion cussì ardide, cussì assurde, e profitâ da la disponibilitât da lis dôs feminis. O ai a cûr il moment di Amlêt, e nancje par zûc mi sint di dâ seont al desideri des dôs inglesis, cussì mecanic, cence passion.

Dopo vê finît il burger e une sorsade di bire, mi alci cun educazion par no dâ lûc a coments soradins, e o fâs segn a Amlêt di seguîmi viers la puarte. Il zovin mi ven daûr cence dî nuie, e al lasse burger e bire su la taule.

'I talians a smucin vie … Sborâts di latin lovers!'

Espression compagnade dal ridi sarcastic da lis dôs feminis che no si imagjinavin un finâl cussì inspietât.

VIERS HAMPSTEAD GREEN

Al è cuasi scûr cuant che o rivìn difûr. O ai di gnûf di inventâmi alc par dâ un sens a une zornade cussì dificile.
Nûi sburîts dal Atlantic a passin denant di une sesulute di lune che si è a pene alçade parsore lis cjasis. La serade e je plasevule. Si sta ben difûr. No sin lontan di Hampstead Heath, dulà che o passavi une ore prime di tacâ il turni di dopomisdì tal pub. Un cuart d'ore a pît par rivâ a Parliament Hill Viewpoint, dulà che la viste di Londre e je magnifiche. Là sù, sentât suntune bancjine, o jeri solit passâ il timp a lei o a scrivi da la mê nostalgjie di cjase, da la lontananance dai amîs.
O cjapìn la strade plui curte par Hampstead Green, cuant che l'orloi dal tor da la glesie di Saint Stephen's Rosslyn Hill al bat lis dîs. Amlêt al è cumò une vore solevât, e mi ven daûr content di chest nestri pelegrinâ par Londre di gnot.
In chê zone trancuile di Londre si cjamine ben. No je restade plui tante int in zîr, dome cualchi biele di gnot denant dai ambients noturnis, e raris personis che a tornin cjase di vore, da la cjaminade cul cjan, dai divertiments intune Londre pôc frecuentade dai turiscj.
O jentrìn dentri il parc, e o lin par un tocut di rive sù, viers Parliament Hill Viewpoint. Mi impensi inmò da lis bancjinis cuntune viste sterminade su lis lûs da la citât tal scûr da la gnot. O ai un ricuart bielissim di cuant che dopo il lavôr, dopo lis undis di sere, o jeri finît fin là sù cu la morosute che o vevi a Londre. Un altri mont, altre int, une valîs plene di siums, sentât suntune bancjine, abraçât al gno amôr, tal centri di Hampstead Park sul fâsi da la gnot. Lis lûs di Londre là jù insom a meridion, un scjap di stelis

che a cimiin in cîl parsore la grande citât. Come tornâ frut, e no rivâ a contâlis dutis lis stelis sui dêts da la man, o viodimi fantacin, distirât su la jerbe umide di rosade, a scrutinâ il cîl avostan, la ploie di stelis, un lusignâ tal firmament, cuntun pugnut di desideris che si fruçonin lontan. Un frut mai cressût, un cjâf plen di siums, la pôre di frontâ la vite cence la sigurece di un pari li dongje che ti acompagne a la scuvierte dal mont. Insiemi a cucâ il sfulminâ di stelis avostanis, cussì lontanis in cîl, a la fin dal istât.

Strani che propit jo che o varès volût deventâ pari, o varès volût vê un fî, mi cjati cumò a fâ di pari a chest puar zovin, a Amlêt, dispierdût tal so mont, dispierdût intune Londre foreste. Nô doi sentâts achì su la stesse bancjine a distance di vincj agns, a viodi la ploie di stelis avostanis.

'Amlêt, cuant che jo o vevi la tô etât, o vignivi dispès propit tal stes puest dulà che o sin sentâts cumò, a Parliament Hill Viewpoint …'

'No soi mai stât ca sù tal gno torzeonâ salvadi par Londre dai ultins mês. No mi è mai capitât di vignî fin ca sù.'

'Sigûr. Par solit lis agjenziis turistichis a promovin dome il West End di Londre e la City, e al è li che si intropin ducj i turiscj, al è li che si disvilupin ducj i afârs, legâi e ilegâi.'

'Nol è just,' mi dîs. Forsi inmagât dal puest, da la trancuilitât da la gnot, dal cimiâ da lis lûs lontanis, Amlêt al sta a sintîmi, al è li presint, e no pelegrin tal so mont lontan e discognossût.

'Se tu vuelis cognossi la vere Londre,' i conti, 'tu âs di vignî ca sù a nord, e par stradutis fin a Hampstead Heath, come che o vin fat nô usgnot.'

'Lontan di ducj? Di bessôl? No sai se mi plâs ... Insom, o ai gust di pierdimi tra la int. Int anonime che no ti cjale cun suspiet, no ti judiche e no ti fâs pensâ di jessi diferent.'

'Sigûr. La int e je in sorte. Ma distès ta la Grande Londre puescj come Hampstead no pierdin il contat cu la nestre vere nature, ti invidin a la polse, ti fasin considerâ il to stât presint, cui che tu sês e dulà che tu stâs lant. E al è ancje plui facil che tu cjatis cualchidun che al pues dâti une man.'

'O ti fâs passâ par mat ... No sai ce che ur fâs crodi di jessi superiôrs, di judicâ ...'

'No sta crodi, Amlêt, o vin dispès prejudizis parcè che no cognossìn avonde ben nô stes, e no vin timp di cognossi chei altris, di sintî il contat di chei che nus stan dongje ... Par superficialitât … Al è di li che o vin di partî.'

'No soi tant sigûr.'

'Crodimi! E je une fortune se tu cjatis cualchidun che al sta a sintîti, pront a dâti une man te bisugne.'

Al ven daûr un lunc cidinôr cun dome il rumôr lontan da la citât che al va cuietantsi.

'Usgnot, o ai tant plasê di jessi culì cun te e no di bessôl, dopo la delusion dal professôr Brough.'

'Chê li mi somee une robe cussì ridicule! Ce jentrial Shakespeare cun Cjamìn e il Comitât?'

'Se tu lu pensis ancje tu …' Mi straten par no dî un sproposit. Dopo une curte pause o continui. 'Seont la teorie dal Comitât pal Amlêt Furlan, Shakespeare al cognosseve ben la storie dai marchês trevisans, e par dâ sostance a la lôr convinzion, si son inventâts il studi dal professôr Brough.'

'Al è di scometi che a àn tirât dentri ancje me tal lôr dissen,' mi dîs Amlêt.

'Sigûr! Te e il puar professôr anzian che, come che o vin viodût, nol è in grât di confermâ nuie.'

'A àn vût ce che si meretin!'

'Distès, par ce che mi rivuarde, chest câs mi à cambiât

dentri. L'aiar da la Grande Londre dopo tant timp, l'incuintri cun Horatio, la sô biele storie cun chê frute, la miserie atuâl dal professôr Brough, dopo il passât luminôs di studiôs, e l'incuintri cun te, Amlêt, culì a Londre, un câs su un milion, a vuelin dî alc …'
Dopo un moment di profont travai interiôr.
'No sai se o ai voie di tornâ a Cjamìn, no sai se o ai voie di tornâ da la mê femine. Mi soi sintût tant di bessôl tai ultins timps, e ti ringraci inmò da la tô compagnie. Mi fâs sintî mancul disperât. Nô doi, Amlêt, o vin di tornâ a començâ alc insiemi. Un câs strani, o disarès une coincidence cuasi impussibile, nus à metûts insiemi in chest moment di dificoltât di ducj i doi. Al devi volê dî alc. O vin di cirî insiemi esemplis positîfs par tornâ a començâ. Jo o pensi che al sedi inmò pussibil … par ducj i doi. Horatio al à zirât dut il mont, al à insegnât in dutis lis latitudinis e al è tornât a cjase, e culì a Londre al à cjatât une sô realizazion. Lis sôs esperiencis lu àn judât a cirî la juste vie, e al è une persone contente che a sessante agns e cjate inmò entusiasim, emozions, voie di vivi. Fin cuant che o podìn, no vin di deventâ un numar come il professôr Brough. Fin cuant che o podìn.'
Amlêt nol à capît tant ben il gno lunc discors, ma distès al à la percezion di jessi impuartant. Forsi pe prime volte inte vite si sint tratât a la pari. Al cjale là jù insom lis lûs da la Grande Londre tal scûr, lontanis, anonimis, fredis, e chi, sentât dongje di lui, un om che i domande aiût. Une lagrime inocente e dispetose i cor jù par la muse.

'Amlêt, mi soi cuasi dismenteât che vuê o sin il dîs di avost, la gnot di San Laurinç, e di ca sù o varessin mût di viodi la ploie di stelis … se il cîl no si fos di gnûf innulât.'
'Lu fasevi ancje jo di frut, ma no ai mai viodût nuie.'
'No tu cjalavis da la bande juste. Il cjanton di cîl viers nord-est. Mi impensi che o jeri culì sentât su la stesse bancjine za fa vincj agns. Mi plasarès considerâ di gnûf il timp passât, e viodi se al è ancjemò pussibil vê desideris. Noaltris o sin doi câs disfortunâts. No vin vût tant da la vite. Pensant a dut il gno percors, al fat che ti ai puartât ca sù par mostrâti chest puest dulà che o soi stât ben, par tornâ a vivi emozions che o ai provadis in passât, e pues jessi une esperience che mi jude, che nus jude cetant. Une persone che e sta a sintîti e pues jessi di grant confuart, e pues judâ ancje te. Amlêt, tu tu sês zovin, tal ai za dit, ma distès tu âs la esperience di une vite infelice, passade di bessôl a torzeonâ pai soteranis dal mont, tes perifariis degradadis da la citât, dulà che e vîf une fulugne di int la plui diferente.'
'A son mês che o ziri par Londre cu la ossession di svindic, di rivincite su la int che no mi considere, no mi à mai considerât cemût che o soi, e invezit di dâmi une man, mi isole inmò di plui, mi fâs passâ par un diviers …'
'Amlêt, il to malcontent al mostre un fuart desideri di cambiâ lis robis. Ducj nô o vin siums, aspirazions scuindudis che o domandìn a la bielestele.'
'No jo!'
'Al scuen jessi alc che tu vuelis vê, un desideri scuindût …'
'Vinci la pôre che mi sint dentri, la rabie che mi scjafoie … chel sì.'

'Ve, che ti vegnin sù lis robis.'

'Vinci la continue ombre di gno pari che al pindule sot i trâfs da la tieze, e al continue a dîmi tu sês un falît, un bon di nuie. No ai di stâ a sintî la int, i amîs di une volte che mi cjalin fis cun coioneç, mi ridin daûr, mi metin denant un tai di vin e mi disin: 'Amlêt, continus da la tô parintât cui siôrs di Trevîs. Parcè isal che ducj ti clamin cont, ma tu in veretât no tu âs nuie ce contâ?'

'Ti menin pal cûl!'

'Lu àn simpri fat, di frut incà. Sì, o ai desideris … Tai moments plui bruts, cuant che il mont si fâs dut scûr e mi ven voie di soprimi me stes, e fâle finide cun chest mondat, o cuant che mi viôt il dolfin violât, l'unic princip erêt dai da Cjamìn, pront a svindicâ gno pari copât di so fradi sassin … in chei moments, o viôt lambicâ lontan une lûs, il fuart desideri di jessi come ducj, di vê dirit a une vite normâl, di rivâ a saltâ fûr di cheste preson, di cjatâ un cjanton tal soreli, gno, dome gno, o cjatâ une persone che mi da une man, mi acete par chel che o soi, e insiemi començâ un gnûf percors di vite. Sì, chest al è il gno desideri. Al è chest che o domandi a la stele. Nol sarà facil, parcè che jo no mi vuei plui ben.'

'Mi plasin i tiei desideris che a son par un mont plui just, dulà che al è rispiet par ducj. Nissune ambizion, dome un mont plui just intai confronts da lis personis in dificoltât.'

Amlêt mi cjale cu la sodisfazion di sintîsi capît, di vê cjatade une persone che e sta a scoltâlu. Une fortune che no i è mai capitade prime te vite. Un sgrisul di contentece i cjape dut il cuarp. Al reste in spiete, come par fâ durâ chest moment plui a lunc, cu la sperance che nol finissi mai. E je la confession di un savi, e jo, di psicoanalist o deventi pazient.

'Amlêt, un gno desideri, che mi ten dentri, al è simpri stât

chel di vê un fi. Forsi parcè che o ai pierdût gno fi di picinin. I miedis a cirin simpri mil causis par spiegâ i fats. Al è dificil stâur daûr. O pensi cumò cemût che la mê vite e je cambiade dopo la muart di gno fi. Nol è stât tant un cambiament tal fisic, pluitost cemût che tu viodis il mont. Ancje cumò, a distance di agns, mi fâs rabie pensâ a cemût che la nestre nature umane nus puarti a dismenteâ. No je superficialitât come che la persone comune e podarès pensâ. Par agns tancj di lôr nus stavin dongje, a mi e a la femine, a fasevin di dut par fânus dismenteâ. Ogni ocasion di fieste nus invidavin, par no lassânus di bessôi. I regâi, lis lûs di Nadâl, la voie di nêf denant dal barcon, simpri cualchidun par cjase, cuant che tu vevis voie di stâ di bessôl a passiti di nuie, cence dovê par fuarce fâ alc. La int, i parincj si preocupavin di viodinus di bessôi. Di gnûf la nestre vite e jere tacade a cori cu lis fufignis di ogni dì: il balon, la television, la politiche, il TG … E cuant che mi impensavi di gno fi in braç, di colp, o sintivi un vueit dentri, un inzirli, e la sensazion di sprofondâ intun abìs. Cence une reson, cence un parcè, dome un mecanisim al jere lât stuart, une stupide suste scatade fûr. Inutil domandâsi il parcè. La fede inte vite, in Diu che dut al viôt e al previôt, un mût par tornâ a vivi, par tornâ a lis abitudinis, e meti sù la solite mascare cuant che tu vâs fûr tra la int, e a cjase di gnûf te stes, ta la solitudin dal to ambient. E viodi, tornâ a viodi chei moments come se a fossin cumò. La stesse sene cui stes voi di in chê volte. Sì, chel fat al à cambiât la mê vite. Lu ai simpri considerât un fat assurt, une fatâl injustizie. Mi à simpri metût dentri tante rabie. E ancje cumò a distance di agns, mi è restât dentri chel vueit … il desideri di vê un fi e …'
'Vonde! Vonde!' al berghele Amlêt tal scûr da la gnot. 'Lassimi stâ! No vuei plui sintî!'

Amlêt nol è plui achì. Nol sa ben ce che al vûl dî un pari. Nol à mai vût. Cressût cun so nono, so pari lu viodeve juste la sere tornâ da la ostarie. Une rugnade, mai une peraule di confuart, une peraule di incoragjament, une cjarece. Mai.

'Amlêt, la mê e je nome une voie, une stele avostane che e cole lontan, un sium di mieze istât, une spere di lûs par dâ fuarce e vigôr a un desideri scuindût e mai realizât. Come usgnot, il dîs di avost, in tancj paisuts da la Cjargne a tirin lis cidulis infogadis jù par la cleve. Lu àn simpri fat di secui in chest periodi di mieze istât. Mi impensi di cuant che o levin fûr da la Plêf di Vuart, la vilie da la Madone di Avost, sot la ploie a spietâ l'event. 'Vadi, vadi chesta biela cidulina …' E jù e coreve dilunc il fîl fin al çoc insom da la corse. Une volte no jere come in dì di vuê, une manifestazion folcloristiche, ma e segnave un moment di passaç, l'inizi di un gnûf cicli, sedi une relazion tra un zovin e une zovine, 'In onôr e in favôr …' o pûr une amicizie, un gnûf periodi come al podarès jessi par nô, Amlêt, che no je fasìn plui di chest mondat achì. Mi soi simpri domandât se al fos pussibil scancelâ la mê vite fin cumò, e començâ une gnove … impussibil … Dut câs, jo o tacarès da la Cjargne, chê tiere abandonade, dulà che tu puedis vivi in pâs cun te stes. La biele ciduline che e cor jù sburide a imitâ il soreli, che al soreste dut il procès da la vite, mi puartarès fin là sù. Ce isal miôr di un toc di tiere che te dan par pôc, e començâ a fâ ce che ti plâs, cence parons che ti controlin …'

'Int ch'e parone, ch'e cjale ce che tu fasis, che ti judiche … e je dapardut.' O resti scaturît a viodi che Amlêt al è vignût daûr dal gno resonament.

'Chê int alì e sarà simpri, ma dome nô o saressin parons dal nestri destin. E viodi in primevere che dut al torne a

vivi: i cjariesârs che tu âs plantâts in flôr, la plantute che e
piche il teren par saltâ fûr ae lûs, e ducj i prodots da la
tiere che il soreli ju cjale cressi, fin a puartâju a madressi
tal cjalt dal istât. E viodi daûr di te alc di impuartant
realizât cu lis tôs mans, cu la tô opare, il to inzen. Il sens
di une vite dignitose, libar, intune nature inmò a misure di
om, cui vons che ti cjalin di là sù, contents di viodi la
Cjargne sflorî di gnûf come par vieri. Intune vision
tradizionâl dulà che si torne al artisan, aes piçulis realtâts
di lavoradôrs, dulà che il credo al è umanitari, basât sul
valôr che la int e je plui impuartante da lis robis materiâls.
La int che ti sta dongje, che ti vûl ben … Ce pensistu
Amlêt? Isal pussibil?'
'Come ai timps dai miei vons, i marchês di Trevîs, inta la
Etât di Mieç,' mi ribat Amlêt, cuntune considerazion che e
somee vê plui sintiment da la gno.
'Si, tu âs reson, ma cu la libertât di decidi, di movisi
liberamentri, di sielzi cun cui stâ, e no come i sotans dai
tiei parons, dai da Cjamìn, cence dirits, leâts al siôr par
gjenerazions e gjenerazions, cence la pussibilitât di riscat.'
'No jere buine int, i miei vons di Trevîs. Chest lu ai let
ancje jo. Cuant che mai viôt denant, mi domandin di
perdonâju des lôr malefatis, dai lôr maçalizis. E ancje gno
pari, cuant che in sium mal viôt denant a pendolâ di sot i
trâfs da la tieze, mi domande di perdonâlu, di volêi ben a
dispiet di dut ce che mi à fat. Insot, insot nol jere un trist
om … Bandonât di mê mari cun me piçul. Nol à vude une
vite facile nancje lui. Ma jo no vuei tornâ a Cjamìn.
Nissun mi vûl ben a Cjamìn. Amlêt, il mat che al zire par
la roste, e al dîs di jessi un princip.'
'Nancje jo, Amlêt. No vuei tornâ a Cjamìn. Mission
impussibile. I scrivarai al president dal Comitât pal Amlêt
Furlan da la condizion presinte dal professôr Brough. A

Carmela … no sai … e varà za capît … o ai bisugne di timp par pensâ. Tant jê e à za cumbinât in altrò. Di chest o soi sigûr. La compagnie no i mancje.'
Un pocje di lûs e comence a dâ forme al mont dulintor, su Westminster, la cupole di Saint Paul, sui palaçs lontans viers il Tamigi che si piert dilunc la planure in direzion dal mâr.
Jo e Amlêt si cjapìn sù e si inviin viers il nestri gnûf doman, dulà che la Bielestele nus puarte. E zire, e zire e nus guide in puescj dulà che il soreli al scjalde, e la int ti sta dongje, ti rispiete e ti vûl ben. Insumiâsi di un mont diferent, imagjinâ une vite diferente, parcè che nô o sin fats da la stesse sostance dai siums, e la nestre breve vite e je contornade di sium. Nô doi insiemi, Amlêt, Gulielmo, e ducj chei che nus son dongje e nus vuelin ben. Cu la convinzion di vivi il spetacul da la vite fin cuant che al calarà jù il sipari, e dut al sparirà cence lassâ ombre daûr di se.

E chest argoment flap e noiôs,
Di un sium nol è plui vivarôs,
Siôrs, no stait par chest gramâsi,
S'o perdonais, sin chi par mendâsi.

(Sium di une Gnot di Mieze Istât)